SAVANNAH ESCAPADE

A Dottie Flowers Novel

SHEILA GALE

To Dear Cheryl
– thanks for your
wonderful enthusiasm!

Savannah Escapade

Sheila Gale

Sheila Gale

DECEMBER 15, 2016

Dedication

For Lana

Chapter One

"So you're telling me Fred is missing." Holding the cell phone to her ear, Dottie picked up the cigarillo from the ashtray with her free hand. She took a long drag and blew out the smoke slowly. From the corner of her eye, she could see her cat, Muggins, stretched out under the patio table, protected from the sun's intense heat.

"The law firm in Rio hasn't seen hide nor hair of him since he flew to the United States to visit his brother almost a month ago," Arnold replied in his no-nonsense British accent. Arnold had considerable business interests in Brazil. A year ago, he'd managed to pull a few strings and found Fred a job as a lawyer with a prestigious law firm.

He cleared his throat. "Sorry, Dottie. I know this is upsetting for you."

Dottie tried to absorb her friend's words. She looked at the picture of Fred Fortune on her mantelpiece. When the photo was taken last summer, Fred had been forking hay onto a truck at the stables where he worked. He'd turned around and grinned as she focused the camera on him. "If you want pictures, at least let me get cleaned up first."

She'd ignored Fred's protests and snapped several shots of him.

Dottie bit her lip and squished out her cigarillo. "I'm going to try that Savannah, Georgia, number again. The one on Fred's postcard. I'll keep you posted, Arnold."

"Good. The firm's anxious to know what's happened to him as well."

She'd met Fred at Woodstock over forty years ago. For three days, the mud, the rain, the stinky toilets hadn't mattered. They were together. After Woodstock, she hadn't set eyes on Fred until a year ago, when he'd turned up on her doorstep in old boots, worn jeans, and three days stubble on his chin.

He'd held up a bottle of red wine. Dottie recognized the label. They'd drunk this cheap brand in great quantities at Woodstock. She'd invited him into the house where Fred opened the bottle, poured each of them a glass, and told her about his life since Woodstock. He'd graduated from law school in the early 70s and opened a law office in San Francisco.

Growing bored of the day-to-day routine, Fred sold the practice and spent the next twenty years working in different parts of the world. In Mexico, he'd gotten into trouble and served time for bootlegging. After his release, he'd stayed with friends in Western Canada, eventually settling down in Alberta and raising a family. But the marriage broke up. "Let's just say my life fell apart at the seams. I got into hard drugs, drinking, stealing, you name it."

Now he'd hit rock bottom and loan sharks were threatening him. For old times' sake, Dottie had lent him some money.

She hadn't expected to see Fred or the money again. To her surprise, he found temporary work at a local stables and a construction site, and paid off his debts. Dottie admired his determination and they'd become good friends.

Had Fred decided he'd had enough of Rio? Dottie wondered. After flying to Savannah to see his brother Rick, he may have gotten itchy feet and taken off somewhere.

Dottie picked up her iPhone and keyed in the Savannah number. Once again, she got the answering machine. The nape of her neck tingled, a sure sign something wasn't right. She put on her rhinestone-framed reading glasses, picked up Fred's postcard from the coffee table, and examined it. It was postmarked June 14, a week after she and Mabel had left for Europe. It read, *Arrived yesterday but Rick not here. Hope he shows up soon as I fly back to Rio in two days' time.* Was this the result of one of Rick's panicked calls for help? Fred had bailed his younger brother out of sticky situations before.

The doorbell rang. On her way to the door, she took off her glasses and caught sight of her reflection in the hall mirror. Her sallow skin and bags under her eyes accentuated her long, slightly hooked nose and prominent chin. I'm glad I went to my stylist yesterday, Dottie thought. At least my hair looks good. The rich auburn tresses minus the grey, courtesy of Monique, curved onto her shoulders in gentle waves. Although she liked the freedom of wearing her hair down, she wore it in a bun for work and business-related events.

Mabel Scattergood stood on the doorstep. Dressed in a lime green floral jacket with a bright red beret perched on her head, she greeted Dottie with a smile.

Mabel's right hand gripped an overstuffed string bag. "I wanted to drop off some magazines I've finished reading. I've also brought an article on Wales from Saturday's *Toronto Star*."

She bustled into the hallway. "It's a good idea to read up on places we'll be visiting."

"You're talking about next year's vacation already? I can't plan that far ahead. You seem to forget I have a real estate business to run."

"I thought the business was doing well. Besides, you know what they say. 'All work and no play makes Jack a dull boy.'"

"I know. Anyway, we haven't decided if we're going to Wales next year. Or did I miss something?"

Mabel bristled. "The article's worth reading, regardless of what we decide to do. It talks about the legend of King Arthur. I was quite excited to read that Merlin is buried—so the legend goes—on Bardsey Island, off the coast of North Wales. That's close to where I spent my holidays when I was growing up." She began to pile the magazines on the hall stand. Halfway through, she glanced back at Dottie. "You look poorly. Is something the matter?"

Dottie told Mabel about Arnold's phone call. "I daresay there's a simple explanation."

Mabel removed her jacket and hung it on the coat rack. "Why don't you put your feet up? I'm going to make you a nice cup of Earl Grey and tell you all about my fabulous day."

She disappeared into the kitchen. Within seconds, Dottie heard the clatter of cups and saucers. A fabulous day, huh. What had her friend been up to this time? Last year, Mabel had taken a crocheting workshop. She'd tackled the loops of yarn with great enthusiasm but soon gave it up, lacking the patience required.

Only a week ago, she'd signed up for Zumba classes, even though Dottie had warned her the fast-paced dance workout wouldn't suit her. Mabel's idea of physical fitness was walking from her parked car into a shopping centre and back again. Mabel realized Dottie was right as soon as she began the first class and had been given a full refund.

She joined Dottie in the living room and placed a tray on the coffee table. Dottie smiled when she saw a plate of chocolate cookies lying next to the teapot.

Looking sheepish, Mabel said, "There were only four left, and they go stale quickly."

Dottie waved her hand. "While the tea's brewing, tell me what you've been up to today."

"I've been geocaching." Mabel flopped down on Dottie's overstuffed armchair. She looked pleased with herself. "That's the main reason I bought a computer when we got back from Europe."

"I've no idea what geocaching is," Dottie said.

Mabel leaned over the coffee table and poured the tea. "It's a kind of treasure hunt. People all over the world do it."

"How does it work?"

"First, you have to register online. Then you plug coordinates into your GPS device—"

"Hold it! Are you telling me you have a GPS?"

Mabel tutted. "Of course. You can't hunt without one. Mine's waterproof."

Had Mabel the Luddite become Mabel the techie?

"You still haven't told me what a geocache is."

Mabel placed her cup and saucer on the table and settled back in the chair. "It's a waterproof container with a log book inside. When you find the container, you write in the log book. There's usually a little treasure of some kind, like a plastic key ring. If you take the treasure, you leave something in return. It's great fun," Mabel said. "You should try it."

"No thanks. I've enough to do without tramping around muddy lanes and dark woods looking for a cheap trinket from the dollar store."

"You make it sound so unappealing." Mabel said. "And it's not always in the countryside. You can find a geocache in the middle of a city. People of all ages do it. A woman from my church goes geocaching with her grandson."

Dottie was tempted to make a sarcastic comment but thought better of it.

"You've become very negative lately, Dottie," Mabel said. "You keep making excuses for not going out. In fact, apart from work you've hardly left the house since we got back from Europe. And you've only ridden your Harley a handful of times." She paused. "It's that film director chap you met in Provence, isn't it? Hans Van something. It's time you forgot about him."

"Stop jumping to conclusions." Dottie said. "And don't speak to me as though I'm a child."

Mabel sprang up. "I'll say no more! When you feel like being civil, give me a ring." She grabbed the empty string bag and stomped off. As she opened the front door, Mabel called out, "There's a parcel on your doorstep." The door slammed shut.

Dottie sighed. Mabel was right. She had been moody since their trip to Europe. And it was largely because of Hans Van Gogh. He'd taken her out for dinner several times, flattering her with compliments. She'd believed that a romance was in the air and had been shocked to find he was still in love with his former girlfriend. Even though she'd realized at the end what a jerk he was, the experience had shaken her confidence.

Dottie retrieved the parcel from the front step. It was about twelve inches square. She picked it up, surprised that it weighed so little. She took it into the kitchen and put on her reading glasses to take a closer look. The address was written with a black felt pen in block capitals. Relief swept through her when she saw the Savannah postmark. It must be from Fred, as she didn't know anyone else from Savannah.

Humming to herself, Dottie snipped the string with scissors and removed the brown paper wrapping. Inside was a cardboard box, stuffed with Styrofoam pellets. She felt around the pellets, pulled out a small velvet box, and removed the lid.

Inside lay a man's watch and something wrapped in tissue paper. Dottie picked up the watch. She frowned when she saw the scratched, square-shaped face and scuffed leather wrist band. It was Fred's.

"Had this since I graduated from law school," he'd chuckled when he'd shown her the battered time-piece a few months ago.

Why had he sent his watch to her? What an odd thing to do. Dottie turned her attention to the other item. She carefully unwrapped the paper. Her hand shot over her mouth. A severed finger, bandaged and bloodied, lay on the crumpled tissue. Her head began to spin and she felt her knees buckle. Dottie felt a sharp pain when her head hit the edge of the kitchen table.

Chapter Two

Dottie's head hurt. She probed her forehead and felt a sticky spot near her temple. She used an elbow to prop herself into a sitting position but felt too dizzy to stand.

The front door opened and Mabel's voice called out, "It's just me. I forgot my jacket."

Dottie called out. "Thank heavens you're here!"

Mabel rushed into the kitchen. Her eyes grew wide as she peered down at Dottie. "Oh, my! What happened to you?"

"I passed out and banged my head when I fell."

"That's not like you, Dottie. You aren't the fainting type. Here," Mabel said, extending her hands. "Grab hold and I'll pull you up."

After a couple of tries, Dottie managed to stand. Her legs felt wobbly. "I have to sit down."

Mabel helped her into a chair. "I'll clean up that cut. If you need stitches, we'll go to emergency. But first, you need another cup of tea with lots of sugar."

"Forget tea. I need brandy."

Mabel took out the brandy from Dottie's liquor cabinet and poured some into a snifter. She handed the glass to Dottie.

As the smooth liquid slipped down her throat, Dottie's head cleared a bit. "That's better."

In a contrite voice Mabel said, "I'm sorry I stormed off."

"You had every right," Dottie said. "I'm the one who should apologize. I'm thankful you forgot your jacket." She nodded at the parcel on the kitchen table. "Take a look inside the tissue paper."

Mabel pulled it toward her. "Oh, my Lordie!" She peered at the gruesome contents. "What kind of twisted mind would do something like this." She looked at Dottie. "No wonder you fainted. And why send a watch?"

"It's Fred's."

"I see. So you think…." Mabel's voice trailed off.

"What else would I think?"

Mabel didn't reply. She peered into the box again then locked eyes with Dottie. "It isn't what you think it is."

"What are you talking about?"

"It isn't a finger. Someone's bandaged a piece of metal to make it look like a real one."

Dottie leaned across the table. This time, she took a closer look and saw something shiny sticking out of the end of the bandage.

Mabel retrieved a pair of rubber gloves from Dottie's kitchen drawer and snapped them on. "The police won't be pleased if they find my fingerprints all over the evidence." She took hold of the silver metal and tugged. It came out easily.

"That looks like part of a cigar tube," Dottie said. "There's some writing on it. Can you read what it says?"

Mabel scrutinized the small piece of metal. "H. Upmann."

"That's a Cuban cigar brand," Dottie said. "My ex used to smoke them. It looks like some weirdo's cut off the top of the tube, wound a bandage around it, and added red paint, or ketchup, or whatever it is to make it look authentic."

"Why would anyone do this?"

"I've no idea. First, Fred sends me a card from Savannah telling me his brother Rick isn't there. Then he doesn't return to his job in Rio. Now this."

"We'll have to call the police."

"You'd better put that cigar tube back inside the bandage."

Mabel carefully re-inserted the tube. She peeled off the gloves and threw them into the garbage can. "I'll phone the police, Dottie." She looked closely at her friend. "Are you up to being interviewed?"

"Sure. I'd rather get it over with."

Mabel made the phone call. "They'll be here within the hour," she told Dottie. "While we're waiting, I'll clean up that cut."

Mabel found Dottie's first aid kit. She soaked cotton balls in warm water and dabbed Dottie's temple. "The gash isn't nearly as bad as I thought," she said. "You won't need stitches. Just Polysporin and a Band-Aid."

"Your first aid training is paying off," Dottie said.

Mabel smiled. "It's one of the few courses I've actually finished."

***

By the time the police left, Dottie felt exhausted. Mabel heated up some chicken noodle soup and ladled it into a bowl. "You need something in your stomach before you go to bed. And I'm staying the night."

"You don't have to do that."

"I want to keep my eye on you."

Dottie smiled. "I guess I don't have a choice, do I?"

She took a sip of the soup. "I don't think the police took it very seriously. They're convinced it's a hoax."

"They could be right, Dottie."

"I remember Fred telling me that Rick liked to play practical jokes."

"But why send Fred's watch?"

Dottie exhaled with a whoosh of breath. "To scare me, I imagine. And it worked."

"How would he get hold of the watch?"

"Maybe he stole it," Dottie replied. "Or perhaps Fred gave it to him." Dottie massaged the back of her neck. "We can speculate forever. I think I'll turn in. Thank God I've got tomorrow off. Cutting back my work schedule was a smart move. I wish I'd done it sooner."

"You've got reliable staff," Mabel said. "And they know where to find you in an emergency." She glanced at her watch. "It's much too early for me to go to bed. I'll watch TV for a while."

***

The bright sun streamed through Dottie's bedroom window and woke her out of a nightmare. Spots danced in front of her eyes and her head ached when she tried to sit up. Recognizing the early signs of a migraine, she reached into her bedside drawer for her medication, shook two tablets into her hand, and swallowed them with water.

As she thought back to yesterday, and the gruesome discovery inside the box, the nightmare flooded back. She was inside a prison somewhere in Libya and heard the blood-curdling cries of a victim as the torturer pulled out toenails and cracked fingers.

Mabel's strident voice called out. "Dottie, are you awake?"

"I am. Why are you yelling?"

"I'm not yelling."

"That's a matter of opinion."

The bedroom door opened and Mabel waltzed in, wooden spoon in hand. "I'm making pancakes for breakfast. Real ones."

"As opposed to fake ones?"

Mabel grinned. "You could say that. I'm making my mother's Shrove Tuesday specials." She peered at Dottie. "Oh dear, you've got one of your headaches, haven't you?"

"I'll be fine. I took pills right away and they're fast acting."

"Are you up to eating pancakes?"

"You mean crepes. Pancakes are small and round and served with bacon and maple syrup."

"Mother always called them pancakes, so the name stuck."

"I like them, whatever they're called, but it's not Shrove Tuesday," Dottie said.

"I felt like making them. They'll be ready in twenty minutes."

After Mabel left, Dottie took a long, soothing shower. She pulled on her black exercise gear, swept a brush through her matted hair, and slipped on her satin mules. By the time she'd finished, her migraine symptoms had subsided.

A fresh pot of coffee gurgled in the kitchen. Mabel had set the table with a white tablecloth, red linen napkins, and Dottie's white china set dotted with red poppies.

"Where did you find my poppy china? I haven't used it for ages."

"At the back of one of your cupboards." Mabel placed a neatly folded crepe onto Dottie's plate. "Come along, Dottie, eat this. I've made stacks of them. You could do with some fattening up."

Dottie sat down at the table. She cut off a small piece. The taste of melting sugar and lemon juice filled her mouth as she bit into it. "I'd forgotten how good these are."

Mabel beamed as she helped herself to a crepe. "Every Shrove Tuesday, my mother would stand at the stove tossing pancakes for hours. At least that's how I recall it. It's one of my favorite memories." Mabel poured two mugs of steaming coffee and joined Dottie at the table.

For a while, they concentrated on the pancakes. Finally, Mabel pushed her plate away. "That's it for me. I could go on eating, but I'll be sorry." She sipped her coffee. "So what are you going to do about Fred?"

Dottie put down her fork and looked at her friend. "I know the police think it's a hoax. I wish I felt the same way. You still think it's some kind of sick joke, don't you?"

"Yes. I do. If Rick likes to play practical jokes, then sending Fred's watch along with the severed finger is a giveaway. It has to be Rick."

They drank their coffee in silence.

The phone rang. Mabel put her hand on her chest. "That gave me a fright. I was miles away."

Dottie walked over to the wall phone. "Hello... Hello?" There was no answer. "Must have been a wrong number." She hung up.

It rang again almost immediately. Dottie picked up the receiver.

"Dottie, it's Fred." He spoke in a half whisper.

"Where are you?"

In a breathless voice he said, "I've been—" The call disconnected.

Dottie slowly replaced the receiver.

"What's going on?" Mabel said. "You look as though you're in shock."

"It was Fred."

"Is he all right?"

Dottie sat down. "I don't know."

"What did he say?"

"He started to speak but we got disconnected."

Mabel walked over to the phone. "I'm going to see if I can trace the call."

She punched in some numbers and wrote on a notepad by the phone. She handed Dottie the notepad. "What do you think?"

"It's the same area code as Rick's."

"So Fred's still in Savannah."

"I'll try to call back." Dottie keyed in the number Mabel had given her but got a busy signal. She tried three more times, then gave up. "I'll try later."

Neither woman spoke for a few moments.

"Fred sounded scared," Dottie said. She slapped the palms of her hands on the table. "I can't sit around here doing nothing. I have to go to Savannah." She pulled out her iPhone.

"I'm going with you," Mabel said.

Dottie turned around in surprise. "Are you sure?"

"Yes. You know what they say. Two heads are better than one."

Dottie squeezed Mabel's arm. "Thanks."

Chapter Three

Dottie booked two seats for Savannah, via Charlotte, North Carolina. "There are no direct flights from Toronto."

"I know," Mabel said. "I've flown there several times to visit my cousin Virginia on Hilton Head Island."

"The flight's tomorrow morning," Dottie said. "That doesn't give us a lot of time."

"It won't take me long to pack," Mabel said. "I'm taking the copy of *Midnight in the Garden of Good and Evil* you lent me. I'll read it on the plane."

"Don't forget your passport."

Mabel stroked her chin. "Now, where did I put it when we got back from Europe?"

Dottie's mind wandered to Savannah. What would they find when they arrived at Rick's house? Maybe Rick and Fred would be there. If only she could believe that.

"I think it's in the living room on top of some magazines. I hope my cleaning woman didn't throw it out."

"Throw what out?"

"My passport. I'm going home right now to look for it."

Once Mabel left, Dottie studied a map of downtown Savannah on line and booked a suite at the Hampton Inn, within walking distance of Rick's house.

Mabel phoned Dottie half an hour later. "Good news. I found my passport on the living room floor."

Dottie knew any attempt to admonish Mabel on her carelessness would fall on deaf ears. "Where is it now?"

"In my handbag."

"The taxi will pick you up at six-thirty tomorrow morning. Don't forget to set your alarm."

"You're such a worry wart. I'll be ready."

Famous last words! When was Mabel ever on time?

***

Most of Dottie's wardrobe consisted of business suits, silk blouses, and elegant evening wear, along with dozens of high heeled shoes and a few pairs of dressy flats. But she'd need casual clothes for this trip. Figuring there'd be a fair amount of walking, she packed a sturdy pair of shoes. Those, along with short sleeved tops, a light sweater, two pairs of casual pants and a windbreaker should do the trick. She toyed with the idea of taking one pair of high heels, a white crocheted top, and black silk dress pants. If they'll fit in my suitcase, I'll bring them, she decided.

To Dottie's surprise, Mabel was in the driveway, luggage at her side, when the taxi pulled up the following morning. The flight from Pearson International Airport left on time. In spite of the inconvenience of changing flights in Charlotte and waiting for two hours for their connection, the women were in good spirits when they arrived at the Savannah airport.

Mabel glanced around the arrivals lounge. "Isn't this charming? I never get tired of seeing it."

Dottie agreed. "It looks more like a village square than an airport with its old-fashioned clock and rocking chairs. It's even got trees."

They took a taxi to their hotel and checked in. Unpacking didn't take long.

Dottie glanced at her watch. "It's only 4 o'clock. I'd like to find Rick's house."

She opened the map she'd been given at the front desk and peered at it. "Here's the street."

She glanced up at Mabel. "Are you okay with this?"

"Of course. With a bit of luck, we'll find Rick and Fred at home, enjoying a beer."

Not likely, thought Dottie, as they began their walk up Abercorn. Crepe myrtle and other attractive vines lined the sidewalks. Dottie breathed in the creamy vanilla scent of wisteria and honeysuckle-perfumed bougainvillea. At Oglethorpe Square, an old man sat on one of the benches playing a clarinet. Mabel dropped a dollar bill into his case.

She glanced around the square. "That Spanish moss hanging from the tree branches is so beautiful. I must take some back for my niece."

"Not a good idea, Mabel. Yolanda wouldn't be pleased. I read something about Spanish moss in a travel book. It's full of bugs. Rat snakes and spiders like to live in it."

Mabel raised her hand. "I've heard enough. I'll admire it from a distance."

Row houses with cast iron stair railings and luxuriant foliage that spilled from the tiny front yards lined the quiet street just off Telfair Square. They found number 424 and climbed the iron staircase. A brass knocker in the shape of a pineapple hung on the arch-shaped door. Dottie lifted the knocker and let it fall. A loud thud broke the silence and sent a flock of chirping birds spiraling off into the sky. As she lifted the knocker a second time, Dottie noticed a small space between the frame and door. She gave the door a gentle push. To her amazement, it swung open.

"What a stroke of luck!" Mabel said. "Why don't we pop in? It can't do any harm."

Dottie looked up and down the street. "There's no-one around. Okay, let's take a look inside."

***

The afternoon sun reflected off the luster of the hallway's pine flooring. The hallway led to a spacious high-ceilinged living and dining room full of antiques. A crystal chandelier hung over the mahogany dining room table.

"This is fabulous!" Mabel said. "Rick has expensive tastes."

"If he's renting, the furniture may be included."

They climbed the narrow winding stairs to the bedrooms. The first room they entered was set up as an office. A desktop computer and printer sat on a large mahogany desk. Wire trays on top of a filing cabinet were filled with neatly stacked papers. The credenza was piled high with telephone directories, file folders, and books.

A king-sized bed dominated the next room. It was covered in a richly brocaded bedspread complemented by gold satin pillows. The deep red walls were hung with oil paintings of low country scenes in ornate gilded frames. A quick check of the closet revealed a leather jacket, several pairs of designer jeans and casual shirts along with rows of tailored suits, striped shirts, and pants. At least a dozen pairs of finely-crafted leather shoes were lined up on the floor. Italian by the looks of it, Dottie thought.

"I bet this is Rick's room," she said.

The second bedroom also contained men's clothing. Instead of hanging tidily in the closet, t-shirts, jeans, and a couple of jackets were strewn over a chair and the bed.

"Talk about opposites!" Mabel said. "It reminds me of that old TV program, *The Odd Couple.*"

As she glanced at the clothing, Dottie noticed one of the jackets had suede patches on the sleeves. Her stomach tightened. "That's Fred's jacket."

Mabel's eyes shot wide open. "Are you sure? Those types of jackets are quite popular."

"He wore it when he took me out for dinner last year. I recognize the blue stain on one of the patches."

"So you were right, Dottie. Fred is here."

"He's been here, for sure. That's all we know so far. Why don't we take another look downstairs in case we missed something."

As she turned to leave, Dottie spotted a small picture frame lying face down on the bedside table. Curious, she picked it up. Unexpected tears sprang into her eyes. It was the picture Fred had taken of her last year when she'd visited the stables where he worked.

They climbed down the stairs and checked the kitchen, living and dining room, and the powder room off the hallway.

"I don't see anything out of the ordinary," Mabel said, as they closed the powder room door behind them.

"Something's not right. I can feel it." Distracted, Dottie caught her toe on the edge of a Persian rug that lay in the hallway. As she struggled to regain her balance, her eyes caught a faint reddish stain in the centre of the rug. "Look, Mabel."

"Is that blood?"

"It could be."

In a layer of dust beneath the hall window, Dottie noticed two large footprints. From their size and tread marks, she guessed they were made by a man wearing running shoes.

Mabel glanced at Dottie. "Should we call the police, do you think?"

"We need to go through Rick's office again to see if we can find something to give us clues about Fred's whereabouts. Then we can decide if the police should be involved."

"That makes sense."

There was a clank on the iron stairs outside. A shadow fell across the window then quickly disappeared. Dottie put her finger to her lips.

"Maybe it's Rick or Fred," Mabel whispered.

They waited for what seemed like a long time but all they could hear was the drone of traffic. Dottie looked through the window. She turned back to Mabel, shaking her head. "I can't see anyone."

"I think we'd better make ourselves scarce."

Dottie opened the front door and took a good look around. A couple of pedestrians were strolling along the street below. In the distance, a dog barked.

She looked back at Mabel. "All clear. Let's go. We should leave the door ajar, the way we found it."

"I'll take care of that," Mabel said.

Mabel positioned the door and followed Dottie down the staircase.

***

For dinner, they found a small café close to the hotel and ordered two glasses of white wine.

Dottie examined the menu. "I'm going for the she-crab soup and a small salad."

"I'm having the daily special—fried cat fish, yellow rice, and red beans."

The waiter served the wine and took their orders.

"What a day we've had. I'm pooped," Mabel said.

"I wonder what that person who walked past Rick's front door was up to?" Dottie said. "Why walk up the stairs unless you're planning to knock at the door?"

"Maybe he got the wrong house number, realized his mistake and left." Mabel sipped her wine. "I've been thinking. I don't think we should call the police. We'd have to answer some awkward questions, such as, why were we in Rick's house."

"What about the blood on the rug, and the footprints?"

"How do we know it's blood? It could just as easily be paint," Mabel said. "The bedroom wall in Rick's room is painted in deep red."

"True. I tend to get a bit paranoid about these things." Dottie took a sip of wine. "You're right, it could be tricky explaining to the police why we were there."

As soon as their order arrived, Mabel picked up her fork and popped a tender piece of the white fish into her mouth. "This is delicious. While we're down here, I must make sure I order grits at least once."

Dottie shuddered. "Not for me, thanks. It reminds me of ground rice cereal I had as a kid."

"I loved all those types of things—sago, semolina, tapioca. And rice pudding of course."

After they returned to the hotel, Mabel settled on the sofa surrounded by brochures and flyers. "Did you know that in 2003 The American Institute of Paranormal Activity named Savannah the most haunted city in America? There are at least six ghost tours available."

Dottie glanced up from her copy of Pat Conroy's *The Great Santini.* "They must be popular."

Mabel flipped through more brochures. "I've found a *Midnight in the Garden of Good and Evil* tour. It includes the house where the murder took place. It'd be interesting to see places mentioned in the book."

"I don't want to put a damper on your enthusiasm, Mabel, but I'm not in the mood for touring right now."

"I know. But once we find Fred, we can relax and enjoy Savannah."

***

The next morning, they had breakfast at a nearby restaurant. Mabel chose waffles with fresh strawberries and whipped cream.

"I thought you'd decided to try grits," Dottie said, spooning Greek yoghurt over a bowl of blueberries.

"I was all set to order them, then I saw one of the waitresses serving this. It looked so good I couldn't resist."

Mabel dug her spoon into the mound of strawberries and cream. "I'm thinking of going on the Paleo diet when we get home."

"What happened to the South Beach diet?"

"I think this one will work for me."

"There's no dairy allowed in the Paleo diet. You wouldn't be able to eat cream with your strawberries. And Dairy Queen is out."

Mabel pursed her lips. "You're zeroing in on the negative aspect of the diet. You can eat all kinds of meat, fish, and seafood."

Dottie shrugged. "I'll believe it when I see it." She took out her iPhone. "I need to check if my granddaughter's feeling better. Hettie and the twins are staying at my place for a few days while their new kitchen's being installed."

"What's wrong with little Rachael?"

"She's had a fever and upset tummy."

Dottie got through to her daughter right away. "How's the patient?"

"You're not going to believe it. She's wolfing down pancakes with maple syrup as we speak. That's kids for you."

"That's great news. How's Muggins? Behaving himself?"

"Very well. He's sitting at the bay window watching the birds. By the way, I had an odd phone call yesterday. A guy called. Said he was a friend of yours. He sounded quite charming. I didn't catch his name. It was a terrible connection. I think he said he was in Kenya." A scream filled the air followed by a yell. "Those two are at it again. Must go."

Dottie told Mabel about her mystery caller.

"It's probably our friend Tom Snead," Mabel said. "He's always gadding about in some foreign country or another."

Dottie couldn't imagine Tom Snead in Africa. Europe was more his style. She drained her coffee mug. Could the caller have been Hans Van Gogh? she wondered. He'd made two documentaries in Africa. Maybe he was working on a third.

In spite of her determination to forget about Hans, an image of the candlelit dinner in the old Tuscan town of Lucca flashed into her head. Hans had been a gracious host, ordering the best wines and dishes. Over dinner, he'd regaled her with tales of his African adventures.

After the meal, while they sipped brandy liqueurs, he'd reached over, took her hand, and looked at her with his piercing blue eyes. "Dottie, I believe we are soul mates." Later, Dottie wondered how he'd figured that out as he'd done all the talking.

The evening was over too soon. He'd escorted her back to the cabana, took her in his arms, and kissed her, with a promise to call. The call never came.

***

Once breakfast was over, Dottie and Mabel decided to go back to Rick's house. As they walked past the lobby toward the front door, the desk clerk spoke. "Excuse me, Ms. Flowers."

Dottie glanced back.

"I have something for you." The clerk slipped her hand under the desk and pulled out a small padded envelope.

Dottie frowned. Apart from her staff and children, she'd told no-one where they were staying.

She took the envelope and looked at it. The words DOTTIE FLOWERS – URGENT were printed with a black marker across the front.

She looked at the desk clerk. "Did you see who dropped this off?"

"It was a man. He handed it to me about an hour ago. He was very insistent that I gave it to you before you left the hotel this morning."

"Can you remember what he looked like?'

"Not really," the clerk said. "I took the envelope and placed it in your mail slot. The phone rang and by the time I'd finished with the customer, he was gone."

Dottie persisted. "Was he young? I mean, your age?"

"Oh, no, he was quite old."

"Old?"

The young woman blushed. "Probably a bit older than you."

"Bald? Or full head of hair?"

"Honestly, I can't tell you." She began to fumble with some papers.

Dottie sighed inwardly.

"Thanks." She glanced at Mabel. "Let's go to our suite and open the package."

They turned to leave.

"Wait a minute," the desk clerk said.

Dottie swung around.

"He was wearing red running shoes. It looked a bit weird with his business suit, if you know what I mean."

As they walked to the elevator, Mabel said, "How do you suppose the man knew where to find you?"

Dottie's mind whirled. "Maybe someone saw us going into Rick's house and followed us back to the hotel."

"Or saw us coming out of the house. Remember the person who walked past the window."

Once inside the room, Dottie hesitated, looking at the small package.

"Probably another of Rick's practical jokes."

"Let's hope it's more palatable than the last one," Dottie said. She shook the contents of the envelope onto the desk.

Chapter Four

A gold ring clattered onto the smooth wood surface. "Thank goodness it's not another grisly-looking finger," Mabel said. She took a closer look. "A man's ring, by the looks of it."

Dottie's breath caught in her throat when she saw the dragon engraved on it. "It's Fred's."

"How do you know?"

"He wears this ring all the time." She sighed. "I wish I knew what's going on."

Mabel sat on the edge of the bed. "I've been thinking. That finger replica someone sent you could have been a ruse to get you here."

"What do you mean?"

"Well, let's assume that Rick knows about you and Fred—"

Dottie interrupted. "We're friends, that's all."

"I know, I know," Mabel said, flicking her hand. "But Rick may have implied you and Fred are... what's that term people use these days?"

"An item." Dottie pulled out the desk chair and sat down, facing Mabel. "Why would Rick do that? And even if he did, I still don't see what you're getting at."

"We know from what Fred's told you that Rick likes to exaggerate. Suppose he's told friends of his that his brother is involved with a rich divorcee."

"You do like to speculate. Even if he has, why does it matter?"

"Blackmail."

"Where do you get these hair-brained ideas from, Mabel?" Dottie sighed with exasperation. She stood up and put the chair back in place. "Let's go to Rick's house." She patted her Dior shoulder bag. "I've got my camera."

"Whatever for?"

"You never know what we might find. I've also brought a flashlight, disposable gloves, a cloth, and a plastic bag."

"You brought that stuff with you to Savannah? Who`s speculating now?" Mabel teased. "And anyway, how would we explain the fingerprints we left yesterday?"

"We decided to go into the house to see if there was any sign of Rick or Fred, remember? We didn't look through cupboards and drawers. Today, we'll do a much more thorough search."

Mabel said, "To be on the safe side, I'll use that cloth to wipe all the surfaces we touched yesterday."

***

Dottie was the first to arrive at Rick's front door.

Mabel had stopped to pat a miniature poodle and got into a conversation with the owner. A few minutes later, she rushed up the steps, out of breath. "Sorry about that. That dog's the image of my Fifi." Mabel paused. "What's the matter? You look frustrated."

Dottie pursed her lips. "The front door's locked."

"Oh, dear."

"I'm sure we were being watched yesterday. Whoever it was must have locked the door after we left."

"Now what are we going to do?"

Dottie shrugged. "Maybe there's a key hidden somewhere."

"It's worth a try." Mabel checked under the doormat. Dottie looked under a wrought iron sculpture of a pineapple that stood next to the mat.

"What's with these pineapples?" Dottie mused. "I've noticed quite a few on houses or perched on railings."

"They're a symbol of warmth and hospitality."

"That sounds like a line out of a travel guide."

Mabel smiled. "It is. The owner of this house has two of them. This sculpture and the door knocker."

Dottie pointed to the knocker. I'd give that a good polishing if I lived here." She lifted up the knocker to take a closer look. "It's encrusted with green - wait a minute! It's hollow!" She ran her fingers around the inside. "Something's jammed in the corner. She jiggled the object until it loosened. "Ah, ha!" she exclaimed. "Look what I found!" Dottie held up a brass key.

"Well done."

Dottie inserted the key and turned it. The door unlocked. Once they were inside the house, she popped the key into her bag. "You never know when we might need this."

Dottie and Mabel pulled on the gloves and began to rummage through drawers and cupboards in Rick's office. They found the usual assortment of office supplies such as pens, ink cartridges, printer paper, and a neatly organized file cabinet. Nothing seemed out of place.

Dottie tried another drawer but it only opened half way. "Something's jammed in here." She tried again, more forcefully.

"For goodness' sake, Dottie, don't be so rough."

Dottie slipped her hand inside the drawer and felt around. "Got it!" She pulled out a brown book, slightly bent at one corner. "We're in luck. It's Rick's Day-Timer." Dottie flipped through the pages. "There are some notes in the back."

Mabel looked over Dottie's shoulder. "It's very flowery handwriting. And hard to read. Look at all those curly cues. The black felt pen he's used doesn't help either." She scrunched her eyes. "This appears to be the last entry, dated July 26. That's two weeks ago. Just a minute… 'played poker until wee hours with Rasta and company.' Rasta. What kind of name is that?" Mabel took her purple-winged eyeglasses from her purse and put them on. "Let's take a closer look."

They pulled up chairs and turned to the first page. When the front door rattled open a few minutes later, they were so focused on their task they jumped in fright. Feet stamped in the hallway. Grabbing Mabel's arm, Dottie pointed to the Day-Timer into her bag and the two women tiptoed across the room.

Dottie opened the closet door. It was pitch black inside. She rooted in her purse for her flashlight, switched it on, and directed the beam around the closet. Some clothing items, still in their dry cleaning plastic bags, hung in the far corner.

Dottie pointed. "Let's hide behind the bags."

"Our feet will show."

"We don't have any choice."

They made their way to the back corner. "Ouch!" Mabel complained. "You stepped on my heel."

Squished against the plastic bags in the stuffy closet, Dottie felt hot and sticky. Perspiration trickled down her back. Muffled voices floated from below and the pungent smell of cigar smoke drifted into the closet through the air vent. About ten minutes later, the voices grew louder and angrier. Someone cried out. Feet pounded across the floor. The front door clicked open, then slammed shut.

They waited for a good five minutes. Finally, Dottie opened the closet door and the two of them listened for any noises.

"I think they've gone, Dottie," Mabel whispered. "Let's get out of here."

They were almost at the foot of the stairs when Dottie saw the red running shoes. They jutted out from behind a sofa in the living room. When she got closer, Dottie realized they were attached to someone's feet.

A man lay on his back, his head to one side, arms akimbo. Saliva pooled at the corners of his sagging mouth.

Blood from a chest wound had seeped through his white shirt and suit jacket. Dottie's stomach lurched. As her eyes took in the grisly scene, she noticed the man's right hand smeared in blood. She flinched. The tip of his middle finger was missing.

Chapter Five

Mabel checked the man's pulse. "I'm no expert, but I'm pretty sure he's dead."

Retrieving the cell phone from her bag, Dottie pressed 911 and told the operator what had happened.

The operator wrote down the address. "Give me your cell number as well. The police and ambulance will be there in a few minutes."

After the call ended, Dottie turned to Mabel. "We've got to get our stories straight before the police get here."

"What are you talking about?"

"They're going to ask what we're doing in Rick's house."

"We could say Fred was visiting his brother and they invited us to join them for a vacation."

Dottie frowned. "They'll wonder why we aren't staying here."

"Okay, we thought about it but decided to book into a hotel. That way, we could come and go as we pleased."

"How did we get into Rick's house? They're bound to ask that." Dottie tapped her lips. "I know! Fred told us where to find the spare key if no one was home."

"I don't see any problem with that," Mabel said. The doorbell rang. "Speak of the devil."

Dottie opened the door. A heavily built man and a tall blonde woman, both in uniform, stood on the doorstep. The man's blue shirt stretched over his massive arms and protruding belly.

They showed their ID's. "I'm Officer Rawlins," the man's deep voice rumbled. "And this is my colleague, Officer Lovett."

They followed Dottie into the living area. Officer Lovett knelt down beside the body and checked for signs of life. She glanced up at her partner and shook her head. Tapping in numbers on her cell phone, she walked over to the window. Moments later, she spoke into the phone, her voice low and urgent.

Rawlins removed a notebook from his shirt pocket. He looked at the two women. "I need to ask you some questions."

He pointed toward a loveseat. "If you ladies would sit over there, we can get started."

They sat down as directed. The officer grabbed one of the dining room chairs and placed it in front of the loveseat. It creaked as he sat down.

He leaned forward and focused on the two women. "Before I begin, would you ladies like to explain why you're wearing disposable gloves?"

Dottie broke out in a cold sweat. She'd forgotten all about the gloves! She snapped them off.

"There's a simple explanation," she said. "We decided to give the place a good clean."

"That's right," Mabel broke in. "We were checking upstairs to see what needed doing, when we heard the front door open."

He folded his arms across his stomach. "And may I ask why you're wearing such fancy clothes to clean a house?"

At that moment, Officer Lovett crossed the room and spoke with her partner. "CSI is on the way."

Officer Rawlins pulled his bulky frame out of the chair. "Right. Ladies, you're coming down to the station with me."

"Why?" Mabel demanded.

His eyes narrowed into tiny slits. "It seems to me that you and your friend here have got a lot of explaining to do."

***

They arrived at the station a short time later. Officer Lovett ushered them into a small interview room that reeked of stale cigarettes and coffee.

"I need to use the facilities," Dottie said.

The officer gave her the washroom's location and Dottie left.

On her way back to the interview room, Dottie heard Officer Rawlins's deep voice boom through an open office door.

"Probably a waste of time but I need to check them out. They were wearing disposable gloves. Tried to convince me they were about to clean the house."

The other person, presumably one of Rawlins' colleagues, chuckled. "They've been watching too many crime shows."

Dottie clenched her teeth. So Rawlins thinks we're two old biddies playing detective, does he? I'll show him. She marched into the interview room and plunked herself down on the chair next to Mabel.

"What's happened?" Mabel whispered.

"Tell you later."

Officer Rawlins lumbered in and settled himself behind the table, a Styrofoam coffee cup in his hand. First, he wrote down their names on a form and told them the interview would be recorded. Then he switched on the machine and reeled off his name and title, Dottie and Mabel's full names and the date and time of interview.

He looked at each of them in turn. "This question is directed at Mrs. Flowers. I'd like to know what you and Mrs. Scattergood were doing in Mr. Fortune's house this morning, and why you were wearing rubber gloves."

Dottie decided it was time to tell the truth. "We were in Rick's house looking for clues. We wore gloves because we didn't want to leave fingerprints."

"Clues?"

"Yes. We were hoping to find something that would tell us where Fred Fortune, Rick's brother, had gone."

"Is he missing?"

"We think so. That's why we came to Savannah."

The officer sat back in his chair. "Okay. I need to know the whole story."

Dottie gave him a brief account of what had led to the trip. When she told him about the contents of the parcel, Officer Rawlins shook his head. "You're telling me you think Fred Fortune has gone missing because someone played a practical joke on you?"

Dottie bristled. "Of course not! Fred hasn't been in contact with his company since he left around six weeks ago. Something's wrong."

Then she told the officer about the phone call from Fred.

"What exactly did he say?'

"Not much. He said, 'Dottie, it's Fred. I've been....'"

"Go on."

"That was it. The call was cut off."

Officer Rawlins sighed. He removed the plastic lid from his cup and drank some of his coffee. "What do you think has happened to Fred Fortune, Mrs. Flowers?"

"Yesterday, a man wearing red shoes dropped a parcel off at the hotel. It was addressed to me and contained Fred's ring. This morning, a man in red shoes was murdered in Rick's house."

"What are you saying?"

"I think something's happened to Fred and I'm afraid for his safety."

Mabel jumped in. "He may have been abducted."

An incredulous expression came over Officer Rawlins' face. He put his cup down. "That's a pretty dramatic statement to make, Mrs. Scattergood. What makes you think that?"

"There are marks on the rug in the front hall that look as though they may be bloodstains. And large footprints," Mabel said. "I think masked men came to Rick's house and grabbed Fred. When he tried to escape, one of his abductors punched him, probably in the face. Maybe they broke one of his teeth."

Officer Rawlins blinked. "Mrs. Scattergood. You have a vivid imagination."

"What Mabel… Mrs. Scattergood means is—"

The officer cut in. "I know what she's getting at, Mrs. Flowers."

He spoke into the machine indicating the interview was over.

Mabel looked at the officer. "Are we allowed to leave now?"

"Yes. But I need to know where you're staying in case we have to get in touch with you."

Dottie gave him the name of the hotel and the phone number.

Officer Rawlins leaned toward them, arms folded. A smirk crossed his face. "Let me give you some advice, ladies You've got yourselves convinced that Fred Fortune has been abducted by masked hoods. My guess is the two brothers have gone off somewhere. Taken a few days' vacation."

He drained his coffee cup, threw it into a wastebasket, and turned back to the two women. "Lighten up, ladies. Go on a ghost tour. Explore some of the old mansions. Walk through the squares. Sit on a bench and enjoy an ice cream cone. By the time you've done all that, the men will likely be back, looking forward to a home-cooked meal."

***

A few minutes later, the police dropped Dottie and Mabel off at the hotel.

"I don't think I've ever been so glad to get out of a place," Mabel muttered as she zapped the entry card to their suite.

"What a prick!" Mabel blushed. "Sorry, Dottie, I don't usually use words like that but Rawlins really bugged me."

"I can think of far worse words than that to describe him." Dottie followed Mabel into the room and sat down on the couch. "Talk about condescending. 'Take my advice, ladies, sit on a bench, have an ice cream.' It's a wonder he didn't advise us to take an afternoon nap."

"You were upset when you came back from the washroom. What was that about?"

Dottie told Mabel about overhearing Rawlins' disparaging remarks. "It's clear he thinks we're interfering old women trying to play detectives."

"If that's what they think, they certainly took their time questioning us. I mean, here we are, two innocents on vacation—"

"We're hardly innocents," Dottie cut in. "We've been in Rick's house twice, uninvited. We've searched through his stuff, and stolen his Day-Timer."

"The police don't know that."

Dottie felt the urge to laugh. "True, but Rawlins knew we weren't telling the truth when we told him we were wearing disposable gloves because we'd decided to clean the house. I mean, would you believe us if you were Rawlins?"

"Certainly not. Look at me, all gussied up in my floral top and lime green capris. I'm hardly dressed to clean toilets and scrub floors."

"And me in my linen pants and white blouse."

They sank down on the sofa, chuckling.

"Of course, dressing up to clean houses could be a good gimmick. Let's think of a catchy name. How about *Fashion Maids,"* Mabel said.

"Or *Dressed to Clean."*

"That's a good one." Mabel glanced at her watch. "It's only eleven-thirty, but I feel as though I haven't eaten for days."

On cue, Dottie's stomach grumbled. "Okay. Let's have an early lunch."

A few minutes later, they were seated at an Italian restaurant around the corner from the hotel. Dottie chose a Caesar salad, while Mabel ordered a pizza. They both ordered sparkling mineral water.

"I'd like a slice of lime and a little ice," Dottie told the waiter.

"And I'll have the same, please. With lots of ice."

When the waiter left, Mabel leaned toward Dottie and confided. "You know, I seldom order mineral water, but I have to watch my weight."

"You ordered pizza with four toppings and you think mineral water will help you lose weight?"

"If I can cut down on what I drink, I can afford to eat the things I like."

It was no use trying to reason with Mabel when it came to food. Dottie decided to change the subject. "How about we take a ghost tour tonight?"

Mabel's eyes lit up. "Are you serious? I thought you wanted to wait until Fred re-appears."

"After what we went through with Rawlins, I think we need a break."

***

They managed to get the last two tickets on a tour that included the Colonial Park cemetery. Once everyone had boarded the bus, the raven-haired tour guide switched on the microphone. She introduced herself as Suzannah, a Georgia native.

"Make sure y'all have your cameras handy," she said. "You can take pictures at the Colonial Park cemetery. When you look at them, some of you might see round shapes that aren't visible to the naked eye. They're called orbs and they represent energy. They're the ghosts of the dead."

"That's the first time I've heard of that." Mabel patted her handbag. "I'm glad I remembered my camera."

"I've got my iPhone," Dottie said, trying to sound enthusiastic. "It takes good pictures." Even though she believed the orbs were a scam, she didn't have the heart to squash Mabel's enthusiasm.

"I'm looking forward to that part of the tour. What about you, Dottie?"

"I'm keeping an open mind."

Dusk was settling in as the bus pulled out of the visitors' centre. Within minutes, Suzannah began the first ghost story. Her Southern drawl fascinated Dottie.

Suzannah told the tale of a young woman, Kate, who was married off to a man called Marcus forty-five years her senior. Kate enjoyed playing the piano.

"She probably played as a form of escapism," Mabel whispered.

Suzannah continued. "One of the indentured servants by the name of Big Joe became good friends with Kate. When she taught the neighborhood children the piano, Big Joe would join in. Not when her husband was around, of course." She smiled knowingly.

"Marcus was a very jealous man. He began to have suspicions about his wife and Big Joe. One day, he found them lying on the sofa in a passionate embrace. In a jealous rage, Marcus killed Big Joe. Kate was devastated. A few days later, she killed herself."

Suzannah lowered her voice. "You can still hear the piano playing in the room where it sat all those years ago."

Mabel clasped her hands together. "What a tragedy."

Someone tapped Dottie on the shoulder. A small man with a shiny pink face sat in the seat behind her. He spoke slightly above a whisper. "Excuse me, Ma'am. I have studied ghost stories for many years. Our illustrious guide has embellished this one somewhat."

Dottie wondered why he was on the tour if he knew so much about ghost stories.

As though reading her mind, he said, "I like to go on these tours to check the accuracy of the tales."

After a brief pause, Suzannah pointed to her left. "We're now approaching the haunted cemetery in Colonial Park. There are over 10,000 graves. Around the 1850s, many people died of yellow fever. The deceased's family would place the body in a sheet. The body would be picked up at night by the death wagon."

Suzannah paused, and once again, lowered her voice. "Unfortunately, sometimes people were not dead, but in a coma."

"They were buried alive?" A young woman sitting in front of Dottie and Mabel said. She turned to the young man next to her. "How creepy is that."

"That's when the practice of tying a silk string to a finger or toe became commonplace," Suzannah continued. "The string was attached to a bell. When the person inside the coffin came out of the coma, he or she would pull the string."

"How would they know what the string was for?" the young woman asked.

"If you woke up entombed in a dark cramped space, you'd scream, kick, and flail your arms. And scrape the wood with your fingernails. I think the bell would get pulled even if the victim wasn't aware of the string tied to his or her finger."

Dottie shuddered. "It sounds terrible."

"Can you imagine how the townspeople must have felt when they heard that bell!" Mabel said.

The bus came to a halt. "If you want to use your cameras you're welcome to do so. I'm afraid the cemetery is already closed for the night, but you can take pictures between the railings. Please make sure you come back in fifteen minutes. We wouldn't want to leave you behind in the dark." Suzannah smiled.

The passengers filed off the bus and spread out along the cemetery railings.

Mabel said, "It's a pity we can't go inside. There's a gate over there, but I expect it's locked."

She began to take photos of the gravestones through the railings. After a few shots, she turned to Dottie. "Why don't you take some with your iPhone? You never know what might appear on them."

Dottie was tempted to say that it was all a load of garbage but decided to humor her friend who was enjoying the whole experience. "I'm going to move down a bit. That way, we'll get different pictures."

That wasn't entirely true. Dottie was curious about the gate. She figured that if it wasn't locked, she'd go into the cemetery and get a few close-ups of some of the more interesting gravestones. Maybe she'd enter the Seniors Photo Contest again if any of the photos turned out well.

The gate was shut but not locked. She pushed it open and stepped inside. Using her flashlight, she examined the gravestones closest to the gate. The epitaph on one of them caught her attention. She focused her camera and zoomed in to capture the words. 'Her afflicted husband and children erected this marble over her mortal remains.' Afflicted with what? Had the woman been a pain to live with?

Footsteps crunched on the gravel footpath behind her. She turned around to see the man from the tour bus.

"Hope I didn't frighten you. I see you're taking pictures of the gravestones. I spend quite a bit of time in this cemetery. I can show you some with unusual epitaphs."

"That's kind of you but we have to get back to the bus."

The man checked his watch. "You're right. Perhaps another time." He held out his hand. "Ernest Palmertree."

Dottie introduced herself.

"Not from these parts I surmise." His squeaky voice reminded Dottie of Mr. Grumkins, her high school science teacher.

"We're from Canada."

He beamed. "Ah, I thought I detected a Canadian accent."

A woman's voice bellowed. "Ernest, where are you?"

"Oh, dear, my aunt is getting impatient. I will see you back on the bus."

Mabel walked over as Ernest left. "What did he want?"

"He offered to show me gravestones with interesting epitaphs."

"Is that the same as 'let me show you my etchings?'"

Dottie laughed. "I hope not."

Mabel held out her digital camera. "I've got something to show you."

Dottie peered at the screen. "I don't see anything unusual."

"Look closely."

Dottie realized what Mabel was so excited about. A white fuzzy blob loomed from behind a gravestone. "That does look spooky, but it's probably something to do with the digital camera, Mabel. Those orbs Suzannah talked about can be created by dust or rain."

Mabel looked disappointed.

Dottie glanced toward the people boarding the bus. "It's time we got back."

Mabel checked her watch. "We've still got about four minutes. I'm not convinced that white shape is connected with the digital camera. I'd like to check it out."

"What do you think you'll find? A ghost having a smoke while he's waiting for us to show up?"

Mabel snapped. "Of course not. I'll be able to see the inscription on the gravestone now, since we're inside the cemetery."

"All right."

As Mabel took close-ups of the inscription, Dottie glanced around. Her eyes fell on a freshly-lit cigarette smoldering at the side of the grave.

Chapter Six

The two women hurried back to the bus. Suzannah smiled brightly as they stepped inside. "I hope you took lots of photos."

They headed to their seats. Before they sat down, Ernest introduced them to a large, sour looking woman next to him. She wore a straw hat with a feather sticking out of it.

"Ladies, this is my Aunt Ruby. My late mother's sister."

The feather bobbed back and forth when she nodded. "Pleased to meet you."

Mabel switched on her camera and began to check the pictures. "I have at least four with orbs. Why don't you check yours, Dottie?"

Dottie clicked through her own. The waning light had cast shadows over the graveyard, and in several shots, she'd captured its ethereal quality. These would definitely be good enough to enter the seniors' photo contest.

"Oh, my goodness!" Mabel cried. "You've got to see this."

Dottie looked at the picture on Mabel's screen. Although it was a bit blurry and dark, she could see the outline of a figure in a flowing white robe. He stood next to the gravestone, smoking a cigarette.

"When did you take this?"

"Right after the one I showed you earlier." Mabel said. "I dropped the camera. I thought it might be damaged, so I tested the shutter button to make sure it was still working."

"And without realizing it, you caught this image." Dottie took a closer look. "He's holding something in his other hand. Looks like a piece of paper."

Suzannah's voice rang out. "From the expressions on your faces, I think some of you have interesting pictures. As we head back to the Visitors' Center, I'll tell you about some haunted homes you might consider visiting. If you'd like to stay at a haunted inn, try the 17 Hundred 90 Inn," Suzannah continued. "A young woman, Anna Powell, heartbroken over a young man, leapt to her death from Room 204. People who've stayed in that room have reported Anna leaning over them before she leapt out the window."

Mabel looked at Dottie, her eyes wide. "Can you imagine how spooky it would be to see Anna at the foot of your bed?"

"I can't believe people pay good money to sleep in a so-called haunted room."

After she'd told a few more ghost stories and pointed out some landmarks, Suzannah announced. "We're now arriving at the Visitors' Center. I hope you've had an enjoyable trip." She put down the Mike.

Ernest tapped Dottie on the shoulder again. "Excuse me." He cleared his throat. "I was wondering, if the two of you are interested, I would be happy to drive you around Savannah one afternoon. Here is my business card."

Dottie took the card. "That's kind of you, but we're very busy so I don't think we'll have time." Not on your life, she thought.

A short time later, the bus came to a halt. After giving Suzannah a generous tip, Dottie and Mabel left the bus and headed toward the hotel. A strong breeze swirled candy wrappers and leaves into the cool night air. Dottie zipped up her jacket.

Mabel struggled to keep up with her friend's long strides. "I'm wondering about that man in the picture. It was after the cemetery had closed, so why was he there?"

"He's probably some weirdo who likes to hang around cemeteries."

"He may have followed us."

Dottie rolled her eyes. "That's a stretch."

"Think about it. A parcel containing Fred's ring is dropped off at the hotel, addressed to you. Someone must have followed us to the hotel. How else would he know where we were staying?"

"If the person who was murdered in Rick's house is the man who dropped off the ring, he wasn't acting alone. We talked about that with Officer Rawlins. Assuming you're right, how would he know we were taking a Ghost Tour?"

"Easy. He could have seen us get on the bus, checked the brochure to see where the tour was going and headed to Colonial Cemetery."

"Why would he bother?"

Mabel shrugged. "He'd know the tour was stopping at the cemetery and figured he might get a chance to speak to us."

"It doesn't make sense."

Mabel sighed. "You're probably right, but I keep seeing that poor man in the red shoes lying dead in Rick's living room. Something bad is going on."

They turned onto Abercorn and headed to Oglethorpe Square. Out of the corner of her eye, Dottie noticed a man limping toward them, head and shoulders bent forward. He paused for a few moments then sat down on a bench next to a street light.

The street light's beams revealed a shabby jacket and torn jeans. The man retrieved a cigarette and matches from one of his pockets. He turned to one side, cupped his hand around the cigarette and attempted to light it. Dottie's breath caught in her throat when she saw the grey ponytail at the base of his neck. For a moment she thought it might be Fred, until a soft voice muttered, "Got any spare change, lady?"

Dottie sighed. The man's utterances bore no resemblance to Fred's gravelly tones.

Mabel rooted in her purse. She pulled out a dollar bill. The man took the money from her extended hand, mumbled his thanks, and limped away.

"I don't know why you bother. Once he's collected enough money, he'll be off to the wine store to purchase a cheap bottle of booze."

"I always feel guilty if I don't give them something."

A few minutes later the women reached the hotel. As they stepped to the front door a car hooted.

"It's that man, Ernest something or other," Mabel said. "The one we met on the bus with the miserable aunt."

Dottie turned to see Ernest waving from his vehicle and waved back. "Palmertree."

"What?"

"That's his name. Ernest Palmertree."

They walked to the elevator and Dottie pressed the button.

As they waited for the elevator to arrive Mabel said, "I've been thinking. That man in Colonial Cemetery seemed to disappear in a hurry. Perhaps someone or something scared him, and he dropped the cigarette and ran off. I think we should take another look around the gravestone in the daylight."

"I guess it won't hurt. We'll take a cab over in the morning."

"You're on. Right now, I can hardly keep my eyes open."

A short time later, Mabel climbed into bed and turned off her bedside light. Dottie needed to unwind. It had been a very long day. She took a hot shower and dressed for bed. After propping herself up with pillows, she turned on the TV and flicked through the channels. Nothing appealed to her.

Yawning, she picked up a magazine on the coffee table. An ad caught her attention. *HARLEY DAVIDSON MOTORCYCLES FOR RENT.* River Street, Savannah. Since returning from her European trip, Dottie had only ridden her Harley a handful of times. She studied the ad and felt the familiar excitement. How much would it cost to rent a Harley for the day? she wondered. River Street was very close to the hotel. Maybe she'd take a walk down there tomorrow, after they'd been to the cemetery. She snuggled under the bedclothes. Even if she didn't rent a bike, she could drool over the latest Hogs.

***

The next morning Dottie and Mabel took a cab to the Colonial Cemetery. After a rain shower around dawn, the sun had finally broken through. They examined the damp ground. Apart from the discarded cigarette Dottie had spotted the night before, all they found were butts.

As she turned to leave, Dottie's eyes fell on a chunk of broken stone that lay a little further away. A piece of paper had been wedged under it. She lifted the stone and gently removed the damp paper, which was folded in two. She showed it to Mabel.

Dottie opened the paper. The words, written in black felt pen, were smudged. "It's a message of some kind. See if you can figure this out, Mabel."

"The initial capitals are clear. .Haror Town Lighthouse. Meet… 6:30 p.m… 16th.

Dottie pushed her glasses further back on her nose. "What on earth does that mean?"

Mabel studied the paper. "It's the lighthouse at Harbour Town in Sea Pines Plantation. They always show it on TV when the Heritage Golf Tournament is on."

"Where's the plantation?"

"Hilton Head Island, South Carolina."

"How do you know so much about it?"

"My cousin Virginia lives in Sea Pines. Whenever I visit her, we always go to Harbour Town for lunch."

"Let's go back to the hotel. I want to check something."

As soon as they returned to their suite, Dottie rummaged in her suitcase and pulled out the Day-Timer. She turned to the notes at the back. "I was right. Those distinctive capital letters on the paper look like these in Rick's Day-Timer. And in both cases there are circles in place of dots over the i's."

"Do you think it could have been Rick at the graveside?"

Dottie pointed to the note. "Could be. It mentions the 16th." She glanced at her watch. "Today's the 16th. Can't hurt to check it out. We certainly don't have any other leads. How far is Hilton Head Island from Savannah?"

"About a forty-minute drive."

They looked at each other.

Mabel paused. "We'll have to rent a car."

Dottie tapped her index finger on her lips. "I've got a better idea."

"Go on."

"We can rent a Harley instead."

Mabel's eyes shot wide open.

"I saw the ad in this magazine last night after you'd gone to bed. The rental place is very close to the hotel."

"That would be great, but there's a problem."

"What's that?"

"You can't drive a motorbike in the plantation." Mabel scratched her head. "I have a friend, Mary Lou, who lives next to Sea Pines. I'm sure she won't mind if we park the bike in her driveway. Then we'll have to borrow Virginia's car to drive to Harbour Town." She paused. "Could you let me use your cell phone? My battery's dead."

Dottie blew out an exasperated sigh and handed over her phone. "I wish you'd get into the habit of re-charging it every night. One of these days you'll be sorry."

Mabel had a brief chat. Then she gave Dottie the thumbs-up.

"Mary Lou says we can park the bike around the back of the house. It's only a short walk from Virginia's. If we leave soon, we'll get there in time for lunch at one of my favorite restaurants."

"How can you think of eating at a time like this?"

A dreamy expression spread across Mabel's face. "Charlie's L'etoile Verte has the best French Onion soup. And their bread pudding is out of this world. After lunch, we can visit Virginia before we go to Harbour Town. If she's not out playing golf or bridge."

Chapter Seven

Dottie pulled on a pair of navy cotton pants and a light windbreaker for the ride to Hilton Head Island. As she laced up her walking shoes, the phone rang.

It was the front desk. "Delivery for you, Mrs. Flowers."

Dottie's heart sank. Not another of those creepy packages! A few minutes later, someone knocked on the suite door. When Dottie opened it, a woman she recognized as one of the desk clerks handed her a bouquet of purple ornamental cabbages. "Are you sure these are for me?"

"Yes, Ma'am. Sherwood Florist has just delivered them."

She checked the card. *To Dottie. These are from my garden. Enjoy! I've attached a packet of passion flower pills as well. Good for the nerves. From Ernest Palmertree.*

How did Ernest Palmertree know where she was staying? Then she remembered he'd tooted his horn at her last evening as he'd driven past the hotel.

Dottie tipped the young woman and closed the door.

She heard drawers being pulled open and shut. Minutes later, Mabel emerged from her bedroom, wearing floral capris and a bright pink sweatshirt. She patted her stomach. "These pants are a bit snug." Mabel's eyes fell on the bouquet lying on the coffee table. "Who sent the cabbages?"

"Ernest Palmertree."

"He works fast!"

Dottie didn't want Ernest to get the wrong idea but knew she should phone. She fished in her purse and found the business card he'd given her on the bus. She used the hotel phone rather than her cell. After five rings the answering machine kicked in. She left a brief message thanking Ernest for his thoughtfulness, hung up, fist pumped her hand and raised her arm. "Yes!"

"What are you so cheerful about?"

"Ernest wasn't there so I didn't have to speak with him."

They picked up their purses and were about to leave when the hotel phone rang. Dottie rolled her eyes. "No prizes for guessing who that is." She picked it up.

Ernest's high-pitched voice grated in Dottie's ears. "I'm at my construction site. I've just retrieved your message." He cleared his throat. "Wondering if you and your friend Mabel would like me to take you on that tour I talked about yesterday."

"Thanks for the invitation but we're on our way out the door right now."

"Oh dear. I'm sorry I phoned at an inopportune time." He cleared his throat. "Perhaps you and I could have dinner one evening."

"I have to go...."

"Of course. Don't let me keep you. I will be in touch." He ended the call.

Dottie replaced the receiver. "He's not going to be put off easily. He wants to take me out for dinner." She sighed. "I go to Europe and meet a handsome Dutchman. I come to Savannah and meet Ernest Palmertree."

Mabel laughed. "One of these days the right person will turn up."

Dottie shrugged, picked up her purse again and headed to the door.

The sun was glaring so they put on their sunglasses to walk to the Harley dealership on River Street. A muscular young man wearing a black sleeveless t-shirt emblazoned with the orange and black Harley logo sauntered over to them. His right arm sported a full-sleeve tattoo.

"How y'all doin' today?" He ran his fingers through dark shoulder-length hair.

Dottie smiled. "Fine, thanks."

"Feel free to take a look around." Dottie's eyes fell on a maroon bike. Its chrome and paintwork gleamed in the sunlight. "Nice, huh?" the young man said. "That's a Softail DeLuxe." He looked at Dottie. "You know anything about Harleys?"

"I own a Softail. Last year's model."

The man's eyes widened. "Cool."

"I'd like to rent a bike," Dottie said.

"Do you have a license to operate a motorcycle?"

Dottie nodded. "How much is the rate per day?"

"Softails are $110 plus tax and insurance. That covers helmets and 24 hour roadside assistance. You can take out extra insurance for a passenger as well. And a Theft Waiver. You'll also have to leave a $1000 deposit on a credit card." He pointed to the dealership. "Rentals are at the back of the building."

"Do you sell local maps?"

"Sure do. We got a good selection inside."

***

Half an hour later, the two women scrutinized their newly-purchased map. "It's an ideal day for a bike ride," Dottie said. "Let's take the scenic route."

Mabel checked her watch. "Why not? We have plenty of time. It's only eleven-fifteen."

Helmets strapped under their chins, they climbed onto the bike. Dottie turned the key in the ignition, released the brake and eased onto River Street. In less than ten minutes, they'd left the bustling city streets of Savannah behind and crossed into South Carolina. Warm air swept Dottie's cheeks as she drove along the tree-lined roads. In one section, branches had intertwined over the narrow road, forming a lush green canopy. Traffic became heavier as they drove onto 278, the long stretch of highway that led to Hilton Head Island. The island bridge crossed over a tidal marsh, where white egrets stood on spindly legs, watching for fish in the shimmering water.

Following Mabel's directions, Dottie pulled into the restaurant driveway and parked the bike. They removed their helmets, secured them to the bike, and fluffed out their hair. "I enjoyed that. I was beginning to wish the drive was longer," Dottie said.

"It was great fun, but I'm ready to eat."

The flight of wooden steps leading to the front door of Charlie's L'etoile Verte and the porch with its white railings gave a casual but elegant ambience. "Nice-looking place," Dottie said.

They walked in. A cheerful receptionist led them to a corner table. "Enjoy your lunch," she said. "Julia will be serving you today."

After she'd left, Dottie looked around. "What a pretty restaurant. I love the deep blue glassware and the bright yellow paintwork. It reminds me of Provence."

Mabel smiled. "I knew you'd like it."

Julia took their drinks order. A few minutes later, she returned with large glasses of iced tea and jotted down their lunch orders.

Dottie took a sip. The cold tangy liquid flowed down her parched throat. After a few more sips, she put the glass down. "I'm wondering about tonight. Tell me about the location of the lighthouse. Is it isolated?"

"No. It`s in a busy spot with stores close by. The ground floor of the lighthouse has been turned into a souvenir shop. And the rows of rocking chairs overlooking the harbor are usually occupied as well." Mabel put down her glass. "I wonder why Rick, or whoever wrote the note, chose that location?"

Dottie sipped her drink. "I'm beginning to think someone's playing a trick on us."

"You think we're on a wild goose chase?"

"I'm leaning that way."

As soon as the waitress had served their entrees, Dottie looked at Mabel's Cobb salad. "I thought you'd want something more substantial like the sirloin steak sandwich."

"I'm leaving room for the bread pudding dessert I told you about." Mabel pierced a slice of avocado with her fork. "After lunch, I'll phone Virginia."

"Tell me more about your cousin," Dottie said. "You mentioned she's quite a bit younger than you. Is she married?"

"Austin died about five years ago, shortly after they came to live in Hilton Head."

"What about siblings?"

"She has an older sister but they didn't grow up together. My Uncle Travis died when the girls were little. Aunt Gracie suffered poor health. Bringing up two young children by herself was too much. Scarlett went to live with her grandparents in New York, and Virginia stayed behind with her mother in Auburn ,Georgia."

"Virginia's sister is called Scarlett?"

Yes. Auntie Gracie was a big *Gone with the Wind* fan."

Dottie dabbed her mouth with the napkin. "That curried shrimp was divine. So, what's Virginia like, apart from being keen on golf and bridge?"

"She's a bit different. Let's order dessert and I'll tell you what I mean."

Dottie chose fresh berries while Mabel ordered the bread pudding with crème anglaise.

"So how is Virginia different?"

"For one thing, her garden's so overgrown you half expect a wild creature to leap out at you. Virginia is convinced it's haunted."

The waitress arrived with their desserts. "I see why you ordered a Cobb salad," Dottie said, her eyes fixed on the generous serving of bread budding smothered in thick cream.

Once the waitress had left, Mabel continued. "Austin was an avid gardener. Virginia doesn't enjoy things like pruning and keeping the garden tidy, which is why it's become so overgrown. And she never puts her tools away. About a month ago, around midnight, she heard snapping sounds, like twigs breaking," Mabel said, filling her spoon with cream. "She went outside to check and swears she saw a white ghost-like figure disappearing into the bushes. Another time, she'd left the garden shovel leaning against the back wall. One night she heard this loud crash. She found the shovel lying on the ground and saw this same figure disappearing into the foliage."

Dottie popped a raspberry into her mouth. This paranormal nonsense seemed to fascinate a lot of people.

"And she reads tarot cards," Mabel said as she tucked into the bread pudding. "She got an iPad recently so now she reads them online."

"She sounds interesting. I look forward to meeting her."

Once Mabel finished her dessert, she walked outside the restaurant to make the call on Dottie's cell phone. When she returned, she looked worried.

"Something wrong?"

"Virginia's had an accident. She was out in the garden last night, fell over a rake and broke her arm."

"Oh. No. She must be in a lot of pain. I guess she won't feel like company."

"She's stuck in the house and can't drive. She'd love to see us," Mabel said. "Scarlett is expected to arrive later today and plans to stay until Virginia's able to cope."

"I'm sure Virginia's pleased about that."

"Yes and no. Virginia's a smoker. Whenever Scarlett visits, she plays the big sister role and nags Virginia about the dangers of smoking. She picks up brochures from health clinics, stuff like that. They usually end up having a big argument."

Once they'd paid their bill, they rode to Mabel's friend's house. Dottie parked the bike at the back of the house, as Mary Lou had suggested. The two women walked over to Sea Pines plantation and headed to Virginia's place. Tall lush trees and thick bushes on either side of the road provided respite from the afternoon sun. People walked, jogged or cycled along the pathways. Through the occasional gap in foliage, Dottie saw alligators basking in the sun beside a lagoon.

Surrounded by trees and bushes, Virginia's house was almost invisible from the road. Mabel rang the bell. For a few moments, nothing stirred. Then footsteps clicked and grew louder. When the door opened, a large black cat shot through the doorway and fled into the garden.

"Rhett – you come back, d'ya hear? That cat will be the death of me!" The woman standing at the door smiled. "Welcome y'all to my home. You must be Dottie." She waved at Dottie with her left hand. "I have to get used to using this hand until my arm's out of the sling."

Dottie stared. With her blonde hair, round face and big blue eyes, Virginia could have been Mabel's younger sister.

Virginia gave Mabel a hug with her good arm. "Good to see you, Mabel. It's been a while."

"I'm glad to see you as well," Mabel said. "I'm sorry about the accident. Your arm must really hurt."

"I'm on strong painkillers." Virginia waved them in. "Come on, y'all. It's cooler inside. I've got a giant-sized pitcher of lemonade in the fridge. Good thing I made it yesterday morning."

Dottie and Mabel followed Virginia into the house. The hallway led to a large kitchen where brightly-colored roosters decorated the wallpaper, tea towels, and teapot. An oversized metal rooster with teal blue, purple and yellow plumage perched on a shelf above one of the cupboards.

A red counter top, cluttered with a variety of kitchen gadgets and a dried-up potted geranium, separated the kitchen from the living room. Dottie's eyes darted around the spacious living area. The scuffed leather sofa was littered with magazines. Books in untidy piles occupied shelves, side tables and even the window ledge. A plate containing a half eaten piece of strawberry shortcake sat on a side table next to a torn and faded armchair, along with an ashtray filled with cigarette butts. Even though the window was open, the smell of stale cigarette smoke permeated the room.

An orange cat slept on one of the multi-colored rugs that were scattered over the hardwood floor. As Dottie and Mabel walked across the room, he opened his eyes briefly at the intruders, yawned, and settled back to sleep.

"That's Ashley."

"He looks like my cat, Muggins. He's about the same size as well," Dottie remarked.

"Poor Muggins!" Virginia cried. "Has he got over his shock yet?"

Dottie glanced at her host in surprise. Then she realized Mabel must have told Virginia about Muggins being kidnapped. "It's been over a year. It took him a while to recover, but he's back to his old self again."

"Glad to hear it." Virginia sat down on the armchair. Using her left hand, she picked up a packet of Marlboros from the side table and shook one out. "I know you're a smoker, Dottie." She offered the packet to Dottie who shook her head. "Not right now, thanks."

Virginia put the cigarette packet down. "Mabel doesn't mind if I smoke as long as the window's open and she's not sitting next to me." She waved toward the sofa. "Make yourselves at home."

They pushed the magazines to one side and sat down.

Virginia placed the cigarette in her mouth. The lighter proved a bigger challenge but eventually it flared. She lit up and inhaled deeply. "Now I want to hear why you came to Savannah. I have a feelin' you didn't come South for the sun."

The two women looked at each other. Mabel turned to her cousin. "You're right. We're here on a mission. And it hasn't started well."

A frown creased Virginia's brow. "As soon as I set eyes on you, I knew. Felt it in my bones. Someone close to you, Dottie, is in real danger."

How does she know that? Dottie wondered. Then she remembered Virginia liked to dabble in the occult.

"I'd like to help if I can," Virginia said.

"I don't see how," Dottie said, then realized she sounded impolite. "I appreciate your wanting to help, but what could you do?"

Virginia sat forward in the armchair, her eyes focused on Dottie. "Start by telling me everythin' that's happened."

Why not? It wouldn't hurt to tell Virginia what brought them here. "A few weeks ago, I received a postcard from Savannah. It was from a friend, Fred Fortune, who was staying at his brother's house. The company he works for in Rio hasn't heard from him since he left about six weeks ago. He came to Savannah because he was worried his kid brother Rick had got himself into trouble."

Virginia sat up straight. She opened her mouth as though she were about to speak, then closed it again.

Dottie frowned. "Is something wrong, Virginia?"

Virginia shook herself and turned back to Dottie. She rested the cigarette on her ashtray. "No. It's just....I've known Rick Fortune for years. He can charm the birds off the trees. Unfortunately, he has a weakness for get-rich-quick schemes." She paused. "This time, he's in very serious trouble."

"What kind of trouble?"

"A crime syndicate. A while back he got into illegal gambling and lost a lot of money. He was offered the chance to get out of his financial problems."

"By the syndicate."

Virginia nodded. "Rick works for a pharmaceutical company. They wanted him to hack into the computer system. Be a black hat."

Mabel looked puzzled. "A black hat?"

"Like the villain in an old Western."

"As opposed to the good guy who wears a white hat."

"You got it."

"How do you know all this?" Mabel asked.

"From Rick. It started about two months ago. Because he's always goin' on about computers, they thought he was a computer geek. He told them he wasn't capable of hacking into the system. Things went quiet for a while then he was threatened by some crook called Rasta. This Rasta didn't believe Rick. Rick was scared as a cat in a dog pound."

Where had Dottie heard that name? Rick's diary, that was it. He was a poker crony of Rick's.

Virginia picked up the cigarette, tapped the ash into the tray and took a long drag. "He's been lyin' low ever since. He's left a coupla phone messages lettin' me know he's okay, but I haven't set eyes on him for over a month."

Dottie's heart began to race. "You mean this syndicate you're talking about, they're killers?"

"Yes. And after they murder someone, they slice off the tip of the victim's middle finger."

An image of the man in red shoes flashed into Dottie's mind. "Why?"

"So whoever finds the body will know the River Ghosts were responsible."

Chapter Eight

"This same group may have something to do with Fred's disappearance." Dottie told Virginia about the parcel containing the fake finger.

"Finding a finger—even though it wasn't real—would sure make me take notice. Who would play a practical joke like that?"

"It could be Rick."

Virginia's eyes narrowed. "What makes you think it's him?"

"Fred told me his brother likes playing practical jokes."

"That's true, but he wouldn't dare play a trick like that on you. Fred would be down on him like a ton of bricks." Virginia took a long drag on her cigarette and exhaled a ribbon of smoke. "So you're tellin' me the law firm that Fred works for hasn't heard from him since he left Rio?"

"That's right."

"What do you think's happened to Fred?"

Mabel spoke up. "This gang—the River Ghosts—could have kidnapped him."

Virginia's raised her eyebrows. "Is that what you're thinkin', Dottie?"

Dottie shrugged. "Sounds far-fetched but anything's possible."

Or had Fred taken off again? Dottie knew about Fred's murky past. On several occasions, he'd disappeared, sometimes for years at a time. And he'd spent time in prison. In his efforts to help Rick, had he got himself into trouble again with the law?

Virginia rubbed the back of her neck. "I'm tryin' to work out why they'd want to kidnap Fred. Could be they figure Rick will try to rescue his brother, and they'll be waitin'."

"Or they want to put more pressure on him to come up with the money," Mabel said.

"I'll do all I can to help you," Virginia said. "But first things first. Mabel, would you mind servin' up that pecan pie. It'll go nicely with the lemonade. I took it out of the freezer soon as I knew you were visitin'."

"You know I can't resist," Mabel said as she walked over to the kitchen. Within minutes, she bustled into the living room with a full tray and served the pie and lemonade.

After the lunch at Charlie's, Dottie wasn't hungry. For politeness' sake, she cut off a small piece and ate it.

Virginia took a sip of lemonade. "Now I need to know what's been happenin' since you arrived in Savannah."

Dottie explained how she and Mabel had gone to Rick's house, found the door ajar, and went in. They knew Fred had been in the house because Dottie found his old jacket in the guest bedroom. "Later I noticed a dark stain on the rug near the front door. It looked like blood."

"Did you call the police?"

Dottie cleared her throat. "We knew once the police were informed we'd have a problem getting back into the house."

"So you decided to delay phoning them until you'd done a more thorough search." A hint of a smile brushed Virginia's lips. "That's exactly what I would have done. Go on."

"The next morning, someone left a parcel for me at the front desk. It contained Fred's ring."

"First a finger, now a ring." Virginia said. "Obviously, someone's trying to scare you. But why?"

"It's anyone's guess." Dottie went on to explain how they'd returned to the house the next day and found

Rick's Day-Timer. They'd started to read it when they heard the front door click and heard men's voices.

"Eventually we heard them leave," Dottie said." When we came down stairs, we found a man's body lying behind a sofa. He'd been stabbed." Reliving the moment sent a cold shiver down her spine.

"And the tip of his middle finger was missing," Mabel added.

Dottie opened her purse and pulled out a piece of paper. She handed it to Virginia. "We found this in Colonial Cemetery." She told Virginia about the ghost tour and the figure by the gravestone.

Virginia peered at the paper. "This looks like Rick's handwriting. He sometimes leaves me notes if he drops by and I'm not here." Her face grew serious. "I can't see Rick followin' you to the cemetery and leavin' a message under a stone that you might or might not see. Anyway, how would he know you're in Savannah?"

"Before we came here, I tried to get hold of Fred. I left a couple of messages on Rick's answering machine. He may have slipped into the house one night to check his messages."

"Did you mention you were coming to Savannah?"
"No."

"So how would he know you're in Savannah?"

"My guess is Rick figured I'd come to see if Fred was here."

"You've lost me."

"We think someone was watching the house. It could have been Rick."

"If he'd wanted to contact you, it would be much simpler for him to find out where you're stayin' and phone you." Virginia pushed away her plate, lit a cigarette and took a long drag. "Did it occur to you that maybe the note was meant for someone else?"

"You mean someone involved in the syndicate?"

Virginia looked worried. "Yes. I don't like the look of this, but I'm not getting any bad vibes." She rested the cigarette on the ashtray.

Mabel told Virginia about renting the Harley. "We left it at Mary Lou's house."

"You can use my car to drive to Harbour Town." Virginia handed Mabel the car keys. "At five-thirty, there'll be folk around. You should be safe enough. I'll not feel easy 'til you get back, though."

***

The two women drove the short distance to Harbour Town. With over an hour to wait, they wandered in and out of the gift shops. Dottie bought t-shirts for her grandchildren, while Mabel spent several minutes wondering if she should buy a brightly-painted ceramic rooster.

"It's almost identical to Virginia's. It would look perfect in my bay window," she enthused. "What do you think?"

"Mabel, how are you going to take the rooster home with you? It's far too large to carry on board the plane. And you won't be able to carry it all the way to Savannah on the back of the Harley."

Mabel pursed her lips. "I could always have it shipped."

"You need to think about it."

As they made their way to the door, Dottie noticed a scrawny-looking man with a black moustache pacing back and forth near the store entrance. Strands of hair hung limply down the sides of his face and over his forehead. His eyes kept darting toward the harbor, which was clearly visible through the large picture window.

Dottie looked out. All she could see were expensive-looking boats tied to the dock. "I wonder what's bothering him," she said.

"He seems nervous. And it's a wonder he can see anything with all that hair in his eyes."

By the time they'd wandered through the remainder of the stores, Mabel had changed her mind about the rooster.

The two women made their way to the lighthouse just before five-thirty. "Why don't you stay by the shop door," Mabel said. "I'll go around the other side."

"Even though there are people around, I think we should stay together."

"Good point. Besides, if we wait by the door, Rick's bound to see us."

"If he shows up."

"He'll recognize you from that photo in Fred's bedroom."

"That's assuming he's seen it."

"True."

Mabel grabbed Dottie's arm. "That could be him!" She pointed to a good-looking man, around fifty, wearing a blue T-shirt and white shorts. Fair-haired and well built, he strode along the dock carrying a shopping bag in his hand. Dottie's heart began to pound. Was this Rick? Although Fred had described him, she'd never seen a photo of his brother.

A young woman with two small children walked toward him. As he got closer, the children ran up to him, shouting "Grandpa!" He retrieved two small bears from the bag and handed one to each child.

"We know Rick's a bachelor. So much for that!" Mabel sighed.

They hung around the lighthouse for forty minutes. "There's no point waiting any longer," Dottie said. "Let's go."

"Wait a minute," Mabel said, pointing toward the harbor. "Something's going on down there."

Dottie shaded her eyes with her hand. A small group of people stood at the edge of the dock, staring into the water. "Let's go take a look."

As they joined the group, a man's voice rang out. "Hand me that rope, Mike. He's close enough to the dock. I'll tie it around his waist. Then we'll pull him in."

"What's going on?" Dottie asked the woman next to her.

"These two guys saw a man floating in the water," she answered. "They're getting him out."

The men dragged the victim onto the dock. One of them knelt beside him and began administrating CPR.

The woman rambled on. "They live a few doors down from me here in Sea Pines."

"Who?"

"Greg and Mike, the two men who've recovered the body. Greg's the one trying to revive him." She took a good look at Dottie. "You're not from around these parts, are you?"

"No. I'm visiting from Canada"

"We have plenty of Canadians visitors. Golfers mostly."

After a couple of minutes, the man doing CPR who the woman had referred to as Greg, stopped, turned to his partner and shook his head.

Dottie walked over to the two men. The one called Mike spread out his arms as she approached. "Stand back, lady."

"Any idea who it is?"

His eyes narrowed. "You'll have to ask the police that question. They'll be here any time now."

"A friend of mine has gone missing," Dottie crossed her fingers behind her back. It wasn't exactly a lie but she wasn't taking any chances. "I wondered...." She let her words fade away.

The men looked at each other. Finally, Greg spoke. "You can take a quick look but it's not a pretty sight." He moved to one side.

Dottie felt her insides churn as she looked at the broken nose and bruising on the dead man's face. One eye was badly swollen. As she was about to turn away, she noticed a small tattoo on his chest. Dottie took a closer look. It was the design of a heart, with two initials, 'R' and a 'W' inside.

"Is this your friend?" Greg asked.

Dottie shook her head.

Her mind raced. Even if she'd known what Rick looked like, the battered face could make identification difficult. The tattoo might help. Did Rick mention in his notes a girlfriend whose name began with 'W?'

As she walked over to Mabel, Dottie saw the man with the black moustache. He stood to the side of the group, his eyes on the body.

"There's that man we saw in the shops." Mabel said. "He seems very interested in the victim."

"Maybe he knows him."

"Here are the cops," a voice called out.

As two uniformed officers headed toward the dock, the man hurried away.

Dottie told Mabel what she'd seen. "The drowned man could be Rick," she said. "You'd better phone Virginia and tell her what's happened."

Mabel made the call and snapped her cell shut. "I told her about the body floating in the harbor. She was relieved when I told her about the tattoo. She said you'd never get Rick near a tattoo parlor." Mabel paused. "Virginia's got a problem. Scarlett was supposed to arrive tonight but her flight was cancelled. She won't be here until tomorrow morning. I need to stay with Virginia until Scarlett gets here."

"Of course."

"Why don't you stay as well, Dottie? There's plenty of room."

"No. I want to finish reading Rick's notes," Dottie said. "I'll drop you off at Virginia's and ride back to Savannah. And I'll contact the Harley people and rent the bike for an extra day. Call me tomorrow on my cell, after Scarlett arrives."

***

When Dottie got back to the hotel, one of the receptionists stopped her as she walked by the desk. "Mrs. Flowers, I have something for you." The young woman disappeared into the back of the reception area. Within seconds she reappeared holding a parcel wrapped in gold paper and tied with red ribbon. A small envelope was tucked under the ribbon.

She handed the gift to Dottie. What would she find this time? With a feeling of dread, Dottie returned to her room and opened the envelope.

The card read: *Dottie: A lot people like the chocolate covered ones, but I suspect you prefer the natural taste. Enjoy! Ernest.*

Inside the parcel lay a box of pecans.

Chapter Nine

Shortly after Dottie dropped Mabel off at Virginia's house, the doorbell rang. Mabel opened the door.

Scarlett stood on the doorstep, a big red suitcase by her side. "Surprise!"

Mabel smiled at her cousin. "You made it after all! Come on in!"

Scarlett dragged the suitcase into the hallway. She ran her fingers through her curly red hair. "What a day it's been!" "How's the patient?"

"In quite a bit of pain, but you know what Virginia's like. She doesn't make a big deal of it."

The two women joined Virginia in the living room.

"Well! Well!" Virginia stood up and gave her sister a hug with her good arm. "I wasn't expectin' you until tomorrow."

Scarlett made herself comfortable on the sofa. She explained she'd been on standby at Atlanta airport. "I was lucky to get a seat."

"I was about to get us some iced tea," Mabel said. "Would you like some?"

"Sounds perfect."

Mabel headed to the kitchen. She placed the jug of iced tea, glasses and a plate of sugar cookies on a tray and carried it into the living room.

The front door rattled open. "Anybody home? It's Harriet!" a voice boomed.

"Come on in!" Virginia called out. "You remember Harriet, my next door neighbor, don't you Mabel?"

"Of course."

Harriet bustled in, holding a casserole dish in her hands. "Scarlett! I'm glad you're here. And Mabel! Haven't seen you in ages." She looked at Virginia. "I dropped by to see how you're doing. And I've made you a chicken pot pie."

"That's real nice of you. Why don't you stay for tea?"

"I will. Thanks. Let me put this casserole in the fridge first. I'll get another glass while I'm in the kitchen."

A few minutes later, Harriet settled her tall thin frame into a chair close to the open living room window and lit a cigarette.

"Harriet, the last time we talked you'd just taken up treasure hunting. Geo something or other." Scarlett said.

Harriet took a long draw. "Geocaching. My doc suggested I take up something to occupy my mind. I've been a nervous wreck since my little dog Bowser got run over by a maniac speeding along the William Hilton parkway."

Mabel served the tea over ice with lemon slices. "When was this?"

Harriet sniffed and dabbed her eyes with a tissue. "A year ago this week. The poor dog didn't stand a chance. A friend got me interested in geocaching. I was supposed to go with her to the Sea Pines forest preserve tonight but she can't make it."

Mabel leaned toward Harriet. "Tonight?"

"Yes. It'll be light for a while yet."

"I'd love to go with you."

"You would?" Harriet looked surprised. "So you've taken up geocaching?"

"A friend got me involved about six months ago," I've been hooked ever since."

Harriet looked at Virginia. "You don't mind if I borrow Mabel for a few hours?"

"Of course not!" Virginia said. "You two go have some fun. Scarlett and I haven't seen each other for over a year. It'll give us a chance to get caught up a bit."

"We'll be back nine thirty or so," Harriet said. "I'll finish my tea and go get my stuff."

Virginia said, "You can use that old backpack of mine, Mabel. It's in the closet by the front door. And there's a sweat shirt next to it. Take it with you. You may need it later."

"Thanks. And I'll take my cell phone." Mabel grinned. "Dottie will be pleased I remembered it." She stuffed the sweat shirt, phone and a bottle of water into the backpack. Then she added two Mars bars she'd bought in Harbour Town, in case they got hungry.

***

With the help of Harriet's GPS, they found two treasures, which were close to the main track. The third search took them along a little-used pathway with thick undergrowth and gnarled tree roots. Harriet led the way. Struggling to keep their footing, they pushed away branches of thorny bushes that caught on their clothing and hair.

At one point, Harriet screeched and jumped back, landing on Mabel's foot.

"What's wrong?"

"There's a 'gator. Look! I almost stepped on it!"

Mabel peered cautiously at the brown bumpy object lying across their path, and laughed. "It's a dead tree! Come on, Harriet, we're almost there."

They found the treasure box with the tracking book and the usual assortment of trinkets inside a hollow tree trunk. Mabel wrote the date, their names and which countries they were from in the little book and tucked the box back in the hollow.

"Let's take a break before we head back," Harriet said. "My bunions are killing me."

They found a log and sat down. Mabel rooted in Virginia's backpack. She handed a Mars bar to Harriet. "We deserve a treat after all that work."

"Thanks. I'll eat mine later." Harriet took out a bottle of water from her backpack and unscrewed the cap. She took a long swig. "That's better."

Twilight had fallen by the time they left the preserve and started back to Virginia's house.

Harriet retrieved a flashlight from her pocket. "We're going to need this."

"Does Duke go geocaching with you?"

"He does now. We were on vacation in the Netherlands last year. I persuaded him to go geocaching with me. At first, he didn't like it. Said he couldn't see the point of driving over hell's half acre looking for a box with plastic toys inside. After a couple of finds, I could tell from the grin on his face he was enjoying it."

Heavy clouds hid the moon, making it difficult to see. Even with the flashlight, they needed to keep their eyes riveted to the path so they wouldn't stumble over the uneven pavement. Most of the large plantation houses were set well back from the road, surrounded by heavy foliage. Even though light glowed from the windows of some homes, many were shrouded in black.

Mabel heard rustling sounds off to her left. When she turned, two dark-clad figures jumped out from behind a bush and lunged toward the two women, their features distorted with stocking masks. Mabel and Harriet screamed. One of the men clamped a hand over Mabel's mouth and nose and an arm grabbed her around the waist. As sticky tape was pressed over her mouth, Mabel could hear Harriet's muffled cries for help.

Mabel kicked backward as hard as she could. The man yelped and loosened his grip. She squirmed out of his grasp. As she ran along the sidewalk, she pulled at the tape around her mouth. To her right, she caught a glimpse of a heavyset man trying to blindfold a struggling Harriet.

Footsteps pounded behind her; she could hear the man's ragged breath as he got closer. Something pulled at the scarf around her neck, which knocked her off balance. Arms spread, she fell backward, scraping the palms of her hands on the stony sidewalk as she tried to break the fall.

Sharp stones stuck into her back as her captor's scrawny frame loomed over her. He placed his foot on her chest. Tapping his pocket, he said, "I gotta knife in here. Don't ever try that again."

From the corner of her eye, Mabel saw her yellow floral scarf dangling from his fingers. "This came in handy," he grinned, tossing it aside.

She picked up the scarf and dabbed her bleeding hands.

The man pulled Mabel onto her feet. He zipped another piece of tape over her mouth. When he tied a piece of cloth over her eyes, she broke out into a cold sweat.

"Start walking." Gripping her arm, he pushed her forwards. "An' no tricks!"

Where was he taking her? And where was Harriet?

Mabel clutched the scarf. As they moved forwards, she brushed past what felt like a hedge and let the scarf skim along the top until it snagged. She held her breath, half expecting the man to see what she'd done.

A few minutes later, he tugged at her arm. "There's some steps here," he said. "Grab the railing, lady."

Another voice muttered, "Bugsy, hurry up, will ya? We gotta get out of here."

"I know, I know. Did you lock the bedroom door?"

"What kinda dumb question is that?"

At the top of the steps, Mabel heard the click of a door opening.

"Get in the house." The hoodlum prodded her in the back.

As she walked inside, the air felt a little warmer. "Now we gotta set a stairs. Get movin'." She took hold of the banister. When they reached the top, he hustled her along a passageway, then stopped. She heard a key slip into a lock. She stumbled as he pushed her forwards. The door slammed shut.

Harriet cried out. "We've been kidnapped! They'll kill us, sure as shootin'!"

"Shut up!" a man's voice yelled.

Mabel was pushed and fell backward onto a cushioned chair or couch. Her face stung when her assailant ripped off the tape. She touched her lips and the skin around them with the back of her hand. When he removed the blindfold, she blinked several times to focus her eyes. Harriet sat on the edge of a nearby bed, hair disheveled, wringing her hands.

Mabel took a good look at her antagonist, a greasy looking man with his hair tied back in a ponytail. There was something about his pinched face and shifty eyes that seemed familiar.

He threw Mabel's backpack onto the bed, dumped out the contents and rummaged through them. Then he turned to leave.

"Wait!" Mabel tried to shout but her voice shook. "What's going on? Why've you brought us here?"

The man's eyes darted from Mabel to Harriet. "You'll find out soon enough."

"You can't leave us like this!" Harriet wailed.

Ignoring their protests, he left. A key grated in the lock.

Chapter Ten

Mabel rushed to the door. The cuts and scrapes on her palms stung as she jiggled the handle.

"What's the point?" Harriet said. "You heard him turn the key."

Mabel shrugged and glanced around. "It was worth a try. I'm going to see if there's any ointment for these cuts."

"The bathroom's over there," Harriet said. She pointed to an opaque glass door with a gilt handle.

After washing her hands, Mabel applied some Polysporin she found in the medicine cabinet. She checked inside one of the other cupboards and found toothpaste, several toothbrushes still in their plastic covering, and half a dozen bars of Camay soap. On a shelf inside the large shower stall stood bottles of shampoo, conditioner and body lotion. Another cupboard was piled high with bath and hand towels.

She returned to the bedroom and sat on the edge of the bed next to Harriet. Blue veins bulged on the back of Harriet's hands as her fingers gripped the bed cover.

Dottie's cure for shock was a shot of brandy. Too bad they didn't have any. A thought popped into Mabel's head. She pulled open the night table drawer. It was full of books and magazines. The small cupboard underneath the drawer appeared to be empty. But at the back, she found a small bottle of brandy and two glasses. She held it up. "We're in luck!" She poured a good measure into the glasses and handed one to Harriet. "This will help us relax a bit."

Harriet looked at Mabel in horror. "I don't drink!"

"It's time to start. Try some."

Harriet didn't reply.

"Brandy soothes the nerves."

"It does?"

Mabel nodded. "It'll help you sleep too."

Harriet looked at the amber liquid in the glass. "I'll give it a try." She lifted the glass to her lips, took a large sip and began to cough. Once she'd recovered, Harriet drank the measure in one gulp. Her face became flushed. "That feels better. Is there anymore?"

Mabel poured her another shot.

Harriet's eyes filled with tears again. "Why have we been kidnapped?"

"I don't know."

"My Duke will be frantic. And he shouldn't be under any stress. He's due for a heart bypass next month."

Strands of hair hung limply down the sides of Harriet's face. Her straggly hair reminded Mabel of someone she'd seen recently. Where? Then it hit her. Even though he'd tied back his hair, their kidnapper was the man who'd hung around the harbor and watched the body being pulled out of the water. What had the hoodlum who'd grabbed Harriet called him? Buggy? No. Bugsy, that was it. She was about to tell Harriet but decided it could wait until morning.

Mabel finished her brandy then glanced at her watch. "It's past midnight, we should try to get some sleep."

"Sleep? You've got to be kiddin'!" Harriet drained her glass.

"We need to have our wits about us, so we can plan our escape," Mabel said. "Why don't you go and have a hot shower and climb into bed? There are loads of towels and plenty of soap. I'll do the same. We'll probably fall asleep as soon as our heads hit the pillow."

What a load of rubbish, Mabel thought. As if we'll be able to sleep after all we've been through tonight.

Chapter Eleven

Dottie woke with a start when the phone by her bedside rang. She picked up her Cartier watch and peered at the face. Seven a.m. Who on earth was phoning at this hour? Her office staff back in Mississauga always called on her cell. Besides, they would never phone before nine.

She picked up the receiver. "Hello?"

"Dottie, it's me, Virginia. Mabel's gone missin'."

Dottie's stomach tightened. "What do you mean?"

"Scarlett caught another flight and arrived shortly after you dropped Mabel off. My neighbor Harriet popped around to see how I was doin' and invited Mabel to go geocachin' with her."

"When was that?"

"Around seven thirty. They were only supposed to be gone a few hours."

Dottie tried to quell a rising sense of panic. "You're telling me she's… they've been missing since seven thirty last night? That's almost twelve hours ago! Why didn't you call me?"

"I didn't see the point of worryin' you last night. There's nothing you could have done. We expected they'd be back nine to nine thirty at the latest. By ten thirty we were gettin' worried. Harriet's husband Duke contacted neighbors and golf friends. Then around eleven Scarlett got in touch with the police. Right now, they're searchin' the forest preserve."

"What about hospitals?"

"The police checked the local hospital and the Savannah hospitals. No-one fittin' their descriptions has been admitted." Virginia gave a long sigh. "I don't mind tellin' you, I'm worried sick."

Dottie willed herself to stay calm. "I'll get to your place as soon as I can."

It took Dottie less than five minutes to get dressed. She called Harley to extend the rental for another day, with the option of a further extension. Then she called reception. "I'll…we'll be away for a day or so. If there are any messages, you can contact me on my cell." She gave the receptionist the number.

Dottie shoved the phone into her purse, grabbed the keys and bike helmet and rushed out of the hotel. As she rode to Hilton Head, she tried to not to think about Mabel and Harriet. But even the heavy traffic and a near accident didn't block her fear of what may have happened to them. An hour later, she pulled into Mary Lou's driveway. She dismounted, secured her helmet to the bike and ran to Virginia's house.

A slim athletic-looking woman wearing emerald green shorts answered the door. Her expression was grim. "You must be Dottie. I'm Scarlett, Virginia's sister. Come on in."

Dottie wondered why Scarlett's accent bore no trace of her sister's southern drawl. Then she remembered Mabel telling her that Scarlett had been raised by her grandparents in New York.

Dottie followed her into the cavernous living room. A breeze wafted through the open window where Virginia sat smoking. She looked at Dottie, her face grey and drawn. "The police are still searchin' the preserve. Duke is with them."

"You said Duke phoned neighbors and friends last night to see if they'd heard from Harriet."

"That's right. Duke thought maybe she'd dropped by to visit one of them, but Harriet's not the type to drop in on people. Duke's graspin' at straws."

"Mabel would have phoned, if she took her phone with her."

"She did take it," Virginia said. "She said you'd be proud she'd remembered."

A lump lodged in Dottie's throat.

A sudden gust rattled the window latch. Virginia glanced outside. "The wind's gettin' stronger. And look at those clouds! There's a storm comin'." She closed the window.

"I'm going to brew some Earl Grey tea," Scarlett declared.

Tears stung Dottie's eyes. Mabel had served Earl Grey the day they'd met, three years ago. A confirmed coffee drinker, it had taken her a while to acquire a taste for its fragrant orangey flavor.

Nobody ate the muffins Scarlett served with the tea. "Let's hope we get some news soon," she said.

As though on cue, the doorbell rang. Scarlett answered the door. Muffled voices floated in from the hallway.

Two police officers followed Scarlett into the living room. After brief introductions, Sergeant Cooper cleared his throat. "There's something we'd like you to take a look at."

He nodded to the other officer. The man retrieved a plastic bag from his jacket pocket. It contained a yellow and pink floral headscarf.

Dottie drew in a deep breath. "That's Mabel's. Where did you find it?"

"About half a mile from here."

Dottie felt her hopes rise. "So that should help you to pin down where they might be."

The sergeant shook his head. "Wind's gustin' out there so there's no tellin' where it came from."

As she peered at the scarf, Dottie noticed dark red smudges on it. A chill ran through her.

Virginia voiced Dottie's fear. "That looks like blood."

"Forensics will test it. Our guys are still searching the preserve. In the meantime, try to come up with some ideas of where the women may have got to. It doesn't matter how implausible, call me if you think of something." He handed each of them a business card.

Shortly after the police left, Dottie's phone rang. Her heart skipped a beat. Could it be Mabel? She took it out of her purse and answered it.

"This is Flora at the Hampton Inn. A gift basket of herbal teas was delivered here shortly after you left this morning."

Dottie suppressed a sigh. "Thanks. I'll pick them up when I get back."

To hell with herbal teas. In God's name, where was Mabel?

***

The day dragged on. They drank coffee, tried to watch TV and attempted to play cards. Around six, Scarlett made a plate of assorted sandwiches and a pot of tea. Everyone ate something, encouraged by Scarlett who insisted it was important to maintain a high energy level. Afterwards, she opened a bottle of red wine and poured each of them a glass. For a few minutes, they sipped the wine, lost in thought.

"They might have fallen into some kind of hole in the ground," Dottie suggested. "Maybe an old well."

Scarlett put down her glass. "If that were the case, surely the police would have heard cries for help."

"I've not heard talk about old mine shafts or wells in the preserve," Virginia said.

Dottie stood up and, glass in hand, began to pace. "I can't stand this waiting."

Scarlett nodded. "I feel the same way."

"If we don't hear back from the police by tomorrow, I'm going to search for them myself," Dottie said.

"We'll both go."

They could have been kidnapped," Virginia said.

Scarlett's eyes opened wide. "You've got to be kidding! Why would anyone want to kidnap Mabel and Harriet?"

"It's over twenty-four hours since they disappeared," Dottie said. "If that were the case, someone would have contacted us by now."

Around ten-thirty they went to bed. Dottie found a mystery novel on Virginia's bookshelf, but concentrating on the book was almost impossible. She tried to sleep but kept tossing and turning. Finally, she decided to go outside. Perhaps the fresh air would help her unwind.

The garden was dimly lit by a pale moon. Dottie found a wooden bench in a corner and lit up a cigarillo. Apart from the muffled drone of passing cars, the only sounds were those of night creatures scurrying through the undergrowth. Dottie leaned back, took a long drag and closed her eyes. The band of tension across her forehead began to loosen. She thought back to the day they'd arrived in Savannah. It had only been a week, but it felt much longer.

The sharp snap of a twig brought Dottie out of her reverie. Rustling sounds came from some heavy bushes about twenty yards away. Something or someone broke through the leaves and branches. A figure stood in the clearing.

The figure moved toward the porch. Dottie rose and followed from a safe distance. She stopped when the outside security light turned on, revealing the tall athletic figure of a man wearing a white t-shirt and light colored chinos. He crossed the porch and retrieved something from beneath one of the decorative frogs Virginia had scattered everywhere. It must have been the door key, because he placed it in the lock, turned it, and walked into the house.

Chapter Twelve

Dottie dropped the cigarillo and crushed it under her foot. Once the security light switched off, she crept toward the porch, hid behind a tree, and waited.

The man knew where Virginia kept the back door key, so he must be a close friend. But why was he visiting at this time of the night? After a few minutes, the door opened and he stepped into the security light's white glare. Dottie's heart missed a beat. Even though she'd never met him, Dottie knew it was Rick. The chiseled features, although more fleshed out, were almost identical to his older brother's.

After a quick glance left and right, Rick locked the door. He replaced the key and disappeared around the side of the house. Dottie bit her lip. The door was only about ten yards from where she stood, but she hesitated. What if Rick came back? The air suddenly felt cool and she hugged her shoulders for warmth. She couldn't stay out here all night. A jagged flash lit up the night sky, followed by a clash of thunder. Rain pelted down and flattened the pansies in Virginia's ceramic tubs. Dottie ran across the garden, lifted the frog and picked up the key. With the help of the security light she found the keyhole and opened the door.

Once inside, Dottie bolted the door and discarded her wet shoes. She made a mental note to put the key back under the frog in the morning. Shivering from the cold and wet, she rooted in the closet, found an old fleece and snuggled into it.

After Rick's nocturnal visit, Dottie half expected to see Virginia up and about, but loud snoring from the master bedroom put that thought to rest. Dottie decided to brew some tea and made her way to the kitchen. As she waited for the kettle to boil, she tapped her fingers on the countertop and thought about Rick. He couldn't have been in the house for more than five minutes. What was he doing there?

Dottie cradled the mug and made her way to the living room. The glow from a night light helped her to cross the room without tripping over Virginia's discarded magazines and books. She switched on the side table lamp. A piece of lined paper, folded in two, lay across a pile of books on the coffee table. The word *GINNY* had been scrawled across the page with a black marker. Dottie sat down on the sofa and sipped her tea. Her eyes kept wandering to the folded page.

A sudden gust of wind through the living room window blew the paper onto the floor. Dottie saw it had partially unfolded and recognized Rick's distinctive writing from the notebook she'd found in his office. She picked up the paper, grabbed a pair of Virginia's reading glasses, and read the message.

Ginny: Dropped by around eleven. Surprised you were already in bed. Didn't want to disturb you but was tempted. Things are heating up and I need to talk with you. Will try to drop by tomorrow evening, but it's getting more difficult. Rick.

Dottie re-read the message. What did Rick mean by *things are heating up?* Was he referring to the fact that he was on the run? Did it relate to Fred's disappearance, or Mabel and Harriet's? Or both?

And what about his remarks about not wishing to disturb Virginia but being tempted? It sounded as though they were more than just good friends.

Dottie gritted her teeth. The blasted note brought up more questions than answers. She'd speak with Virginia first thing in the morning. After replacing the note, Dottie returned to the kitchen and poured the remainder of the tea down the sink.

Chapter Thirteen

The next morning, Mabel woke to muffled sobs. "Harriet, are you all right?"

Harriet emerged from beneath the duvet with tear-stained cheeks and red-rimmed eyes. "No, I'm not!" She burst into tears again.

"Pull yourself together," Mabel ordered. "If we want to escape we've got to have our wits about us."

Harriet blew her nose, and hiccupped. "Do you think it's possible to escape?"

"I've got an idea, but first, I have to check something." Mabel climbed out of bed and headed to the built-in closets. The first one was filled with men's clothing. In the second, she found tops, dresses and slacks in a multitude of colors and styles. And shoes. A pair of four-inch black stilettos caught her eye. She picked one up and showed it to Harriet. "This will do."

Seeing Harriet's blank expression, Mabel explained. "When Bugsy arrives with our breakfast, I'll be waiting behind the door. As soon as he walks in, I'll whack him on the head with the sharp heel of this stiletto."

"Are you nuts? He'll kill us for sure!"

"You want to stay imprisoned in this room?"

"Of course not. But that's a crazy idea."

"Have you got a better one?"

"No."

"Once he's down, we'll make a run for it." Mabel checked her watch. "It's only six but he might come early. We need to be ready."

They dressed quickly. Mabel gripped the shoe with both hands and stood behind the door. It could be a long wait, she realized. Harriet sat on the edge of her bed, her eyes fixed on the door. Mabel checked her watch every few minutes, willing the hands to move faster. At 6:45, the key turned in the lock. She jumped. The shoe slipped but she managed to regain her grip.

As Bugsy walked in, a ketchup bottle fell off the tray. Just as Mabel took aim, Bugsy bent down to pick up the bottle. Instead of hitting him on the head, the narrow heel of the shoe whammed into his backside.

Bugsy cursed and dropped the tray. Coffee spilled out of Styrofoam cups and pooled on the hardwood floor. Bacon, scrambled eggs and tortilla wraps fell out of paper bags in a soggy mess on the white sheepskin rug.

Bugsy lunged at Mabel. She backed into an armchair, lost her balance and fell into the chair. He leaned over and grabbed her around the throat; she could smell his dragon breath. His fingers pressed down and she faded in and out of consciousness.

From what seemed a long way away, Harriet shouted, "Let go of her, you scumbag!"

***

When she came to, Mabel found herself lying on the bed covered in a blanket. Harriet hovered over her with a plastic cup and a straw. "Here, drink this."

Mabel took a sip of water and slumped back on the pillow. "What happened?" she rasped.

"He tried to choke you. I hammered him on the back with my fists until he backed away. He soon sobered up when you didn't open your eyes. He left as soon as you started to come around."

"Probably scared he killed me."

Harriet paused. "You were brave. It took a lot of guts to try something like that."

"Not brave, stupid." Mabel managed a weak smile. "Thanks, Harriet."

Chapter Fourteen

Virginia and Scarlett were eating breakfast when Dottie joined them at the kitchen table.

Scarlett turned to Dottie. "Did you go outside last night, Dottie? I thought I heard the back door opening. And the security light came on a few times."

Dottie poured some coffee. "I couldn't sleep so I decided to get some fresh air. I'd just lit a cigarillo when someone stepped out of the bushes and rushed passed me toward the porch. He found the door key under the frog and let himself into the house."

Scarlett's eyes shot wide open. "A man came into this house in the middle of the night?"

Virginia sighed. "It was Rick."

"Rick? Are you serious?"

"Yes."

Scarlett looked suspicious. "Does he usually drop by that late at night?"

Virginia flicked on her lighter and lit a cigarette. "Sometimes."

Dottie retrieved the note from the living room and handed it to Virginia. "I found this on the coffee table after I came back into the house."

Virginia took the note from Dottie's outstretched hand. "Thanks." She glanced at the message, placed it on the table and turned to her sister. "I might as well tell you what's goin' on, Scarlett. Dottie already knows."

"I'm listening."

"Rick's a long-time friend. He's got himself into serious trouble and he's on the run." Virginia gave her sister the details. "Now they want him to steal drugs from the pharmaceutical company where he works."

"Have they given him a deadline?"

"Rick won't tell me."

"I'm curious as to how Rick thinks he can steal drugs," Scarlett said. "I worked for a pharmaceutical company for several years. They're kept under lock and key."

"Rick works for security. So he has top clearance and access to the area where they're made and stored."

Scarlett replied, "He still has to get into the area. If he uses his own swipe card, the computer would record his identity, time, date and stuff like that." She paused. "Still, there'd be extra swipe cards in the security office he could access."

"One thing you haven't mentioned, Virginia," Dottie said. "How did these goons know about Fred?"

"Rick's always braggin' about him. He loves tellin' the story of how Fred became a lawyer in a prestigious Boston law firm and is now a 'big shot lawyer in Rio' to quote Rick."

Dottie said, "Fred was hired by a law firm in Rio last year, but I wouldn't describe him as a big-shot lawyer."

"That's Rick for you, always exaggeratin'. And he has pictures of Fred in the house. My guess is some of these crooks have spent time at Rick's place. Gamblin' most likely. And it's possible they met Fred on one of his previous visits."

Dottie leaned across the table. "You know a lot about this organized gang. I want the truth, Virginia. Is Rick involved in Mabel's disappearance?"

Virginia glowered at Dottie. "Rick's a fool in many ways. But he's no kidnapper."

"If that's what's happened," Scarlett said.

For a while, no one spoke. The only sound came from a dripping tap.

Scarlett stroked her chin. "Do Harriet and Mabel have cell phones with them?"

"Harriet doesn't have one," Virginia said. "Mabel took hers."

"That's a change," Dottie said. "She usually forgets. And when she does remember, the battery's often dead."

"She said you'd be pleased to know she'd remembered to take it."

Dottie blinked back unexpected tears. "I've tried to call her number several times but it goes to message right away."

"The kidnappers would never let her keep a cell phone," Virginia reasoned.

"If they were kidnapped," Scarlett stressed, pouring herself another coffee.

Virginia took another drag of her cigarette. "I wonder what Rick wants to talk about. I hope he comes by tonight."

Scarlett looked directly at Virginia. "Am I right in thinkin' that you and Rick—"

"Are lovers? Yes." Virginia rested her cigarette on the ashtray. "Have been for over a year."

"Virginia, do you realize what a dangerous position you're in? If these mobsters find out about your relationship with Rick, you could be their next target."

Virginia dismissed her sister's words with a flick of her hand. "They won't. If Rick suspects someone's followin', he's an expert at losin' them." She smiled at Scarlett. "Stop your frettin'. I appreciate your concern, but there's no need."

"In all likelihood, this gang kidnapped Fred. And now Mabel and Harriet have disappeared. There's plenty of reason to be concerned."

A while later, as Dottie and Scarlett cleared away the breakfast dishes, Scarlett confided, "I'm worried about Virginia. I love my sister dearly, but if she thinks she can trust Rick, she's living in la la land."

"I agree. These criminals do whatever it takes to get what they want, including murder." Dottie told Scarlett about the corpse in the red shoes.

Placing her hands on her hips, Scarlett declared, "Okay. That's it. As soon as Rick shows up, we're going to have a serious talk."

Chapter Fifteen

Harriet paced the bedroom in leopard skin patterned tights, a loose-fitting silk top and satin mules she'd found in one of the closets. "D'you realize we've been here two and a half days. If I have to spend another night in captivity, I'll go crazy."

Mabel glanced around the room. "It's too bad the bedroom's in the tower. Had we been on the second floor, we could've broken the window, tied sheets together, and lowered ourselves to the ground."

Harriet stopped pacing. "You've got to be kidding! Even if the sheets held together, we'd probably lose our grip and fall."

"It reminds me of Rapunzel. She was locked in a tower and saved by a prince."

"We're no spring chickens. We sure won't find any princes hanging around this tower."

"As prisons go, we can't complain," Mabel said. "And we've had regular meals."

"If you can call greasy hamburgers and French fries food." Harriet blew out a long sigh.

Mabel gritted her teeth. *If she goes on like this much longer, I'll scream.*

Harriet ran her fingers through her untidy grey hair. "When is Bugsy going to bring those cigarettes I asked for?"

"He'll never give you any."

"Why not?"

"Can you see him giving you a lighter or matches?"

Harriet chewed her thumb. 'I'm going crazy for a smoke. I need something to calm me down." A frown creased her forehead. "Maybe I could persuade him to get me some Nicorette gum."

Mabel did her exercise routine again, finishing off with intense running in place.

"That's the third time this morning you've gone through this!" Harriet grumbled. "Why are you bothering with all this exercise?"

"Blood clots," Mabel said, using a hand towel to mop her face.

"Blood clots?"

"Yes. If you're inactive for a lengthy period of time, they can develop. And sometimes they're fatal."

Harriet dismissed Mabel's words with the flick of her hand. "You take these things too seriously. The so-called experts are always coming up with something. You know what I'm talkin' about. Coffee's not good for you. Then it's the best thing since sliced bread. Wine helps you live longer. Next thing you know it causes cancer."

Mabel took a deep breath and muttered, "If you make one more negative comment, I swear I'll hit you across the head with this sweaty towel."

"What's up with you?"

"You never stop complaining."

"We've been kidnapped by a gangster who could kill us at any moment, and all you talk about is how well we're being looked after!"

Mabel sank onto the bed with a heavy sigh. "I'm just as frightened as you, Harriet. I'm trying to keep my mind occupied."

Harriet sat down next to her. "Sorry. I'm not thinking straight."

A key turned in the lock and the bedroom door swung open. Bugsy walked in. He carried a tray stacked with paper bags and pop cans. His greasy black hair was combed over a bald spot and tied as usual in a ponytail. He wore a grubby T-shirt, with the words *DON'T MESS WITH ME* imprinted on the front. Mabel wondered how he'd got his nickname.

He placed the tray on the dressing table near Mabel's bed. "Here's your lunch, ladies. I got you them salads you asked for. And unsweetened iced tea to wash it down. I don't know how you can drink that crap." He unfolded a piece of gum from his jeans pocket, stuck it into his mouth and threw the paper on the floor.

Mabel took a deep breath. "How long are you planning to keep us locked up?" She tried to sound confident and unafraid even though her legs were shaking. "It's been over thirty-six hours already. And we still don't know why we're here."

"Ya'll find out soon enough." He glanced around the room. "You ain't exactly living poor. You've got a room big enough for twenty never mind two. And them beds with fancy comforters or whatever they call them— "

Mabel cut in. She struggled to keep her voice strong and assertive. "The police will be all over the place, searching for us. Kidnapping's a very serious offence."

Bugsy slammed his hand on the dresser and hurled around, his eyes like slits. "Shut yer face! Or I'll shut it up for good."

Mabel dug her nails into the palms of her hands. Just stay calm, she told herself.

Bugsy stormed out, banging the door shut. The key turned in the lock.

"Don't provoke him. You know he's got a temper."

Mabel's hand moved to her throat. "As if I could forget."

Harriet glanced at the tray. "We might as well eat."

The two women picked up the salads and drinks. Harriet sat down on the edge of her bed, and Mabel made herself comfortable in a pink velvet armchair.

After Mabel had finished eating, she drained her iced tea can and placed it on the tray. "We need to come up with a plan. We should have made one yesterday, but I wasn't in any shape to think clearly."

"That's for sure. You slept most of the day." Harriet let out a long sigh. "I still can't believe what's happened. There we were, walking back to Virginia's after a good session of geocaching. Then all hell broke loose."

Mabel agreed. "The dark road helped them."

"Even so, it was risky. What if someone had come by?"

"I don't think Bugsy thought about that. I get the impression he's not the sharpest knife in the drawer."

**

Later that afternoon, Mabel lay on her bed and thought about the cryptic comments Bugsy made when he'd brought their breakfast that morning.

"You can't escape. You might as well make yourselves at home."

"What are you planning to do with us?" Harriet said.

"Depends."

Mabel had broken into a cold sweat. "On what?"

"You ask too many questions, lady!" He left in such a hurry he didn't lock the door. Mabel listened as his feet clomped down the hallway. Her hopes of escape had been shattered when he'd turned back moments later and locked it.

Harriet's voice broke into her musings. "If only we had a phone!"

An idea popped into Mabel's head. She jumped off the bed, got down on her hands and knees, and pulled out Virginia's backpack.

"If you're looking for a cell phone, you're wasting your time, Mabel. Bugsy checked both backpacks."

"No harm in looking." Mabel tipped the contents onto the floor. A can of bug spray fell out, along with Virginia's old sweatshirt and a bottle of water. She checked the side pockets. One of them had a large tear in it. She pushed three fingers through the hole and felt something metallic. She grinned at Harriet. "It's here!"

"Thank the Lord!"

Mabel grabbed the phone and pressed the ON button. The screen flashed then faded to black.

Chapter Sixteen

The three women sat down to an early supper, but no-one ate much. As Scarlett and Dottie cleared away the dishes, the front door rattled open. Footsteps clomped across the tiled hallway. A gravely voice called out. "Anyone home?"

"We're in the kitchen!" Virginia shouted.

Rick strode in. The wide grin on his face enhanced his boyish good looks. His blue eyes twinkled as he leaned over Virginia and kissed her on the lips. "How's the patient doing?"

She blushed. "Comin' along. I've got two helpers takin' care of things right now, so I can't complain."

Rick smoothed his hands over a mop of greying hair and turned to Scarlett. He took hold of her hand. "You're Virginia's sister."

Scarlett, with her athletic figure and curly red hair, looked nothing like Virginia. Dottie wondered how he knew until he said, "I recognize you from the photo in Virginia's bedroom."

He turned to Dottie. Close up, she could see the pallor of his cheeks and dark circles under his eyes. "I'm glad to meet you, Dottie." He smiled. "Fred has your picture on his bedside table in my house. He never stops talking about you." His face turned serious as he turned to Virginia. "Got your message about Mabel and Harriet. Any news yet?"

Virginia gave a deep sigh. "No. We're hopin' you can help us."

He shrugged. "Can't promise much but I'll do my best. They settled in the living room. Scarlett served the women mint juleps with lots of ice. Rick opted for a cold beer.

He popped the bottle top and took a long swig. "So, fill me in."

"Mabel and Harriet went geocachin' two nights ago," Virginia said. "They left around seven-thirty and haven't been seen since….I'm thinkin' they've been kidnapped."

"Why would anyone want to kidnap them?"

"That's what we'd like to know," Scarlett said. She picked up her glass. Just as she was about to take a sip of the mint julep she stopped. "What about the inheritance from Aunt Gracie? If someone knows about that..." She looked at Rick. "Virginia told you about the inheritance, didn't she?" Her voice rose. "And you couldn't resist telling your friends."

"You accusing me of being a big mouth?"

Dottie said, "You told your friends about Fred's prison time for bootlegging in Mexico, after he'd asked you to keep it quiet, and you've been telling them Fred's a big shot lawyer in Rio."

"What's this? The Spanish inquisition?" Rick took another swig of beer. "First off, I haven't told anyone about the money. Except Fred."

Scarlett's eyes flashed. "Why did you feel the need to tell Fred? It's none of his business."

"I tell my brother everything. And I'd trust him with my life."

"Which you've had to do several times," Dottie pointed out.

Rick grabbed his beer bottle and stomped out. The front door opened then closed with a slam.

Virginia glared at her sister and Dottie. "If you want his help, you need to back off. He's a bag of nerves these days." She lit a cigarette and took a long drag. "Rick has his faults. There's no gettin' away from that. If he sees an opportunity to make easy money he'll take it and ask questions later. And he's not one to keep things to himself."

Through a haze of smoke, she added, "There's another side to him. He'll help friends in trouble, lend them money, give them a place to sleep." She placed her cigarette on the ashtray. "I'll talk to him."

Scarlett sighed. "Just do whatever's needed to help us find Mabel and Harriet."

The front door whooshed open and closed with a thunk.

"Rick's back," Virginia said. You'd better make yourselves scarce for a while. Give me chance to speak with him."

"Good idea. Come on, Dottie. I'll show you Virginia's herb garden while there's still some daylight." She opened the back door and led the way outside.

***

Ten minutes later, Dottie and Scarlett walked back into the house. Rick was sitting on the sofa next to Virginia. Steam curled up from the mug of coffee in his hands.

Dottie looked at Rick. "We're all on edge, worrying about Fred, and now Mabel and Harriet."

His face was pinched and drawn. He put down his coffee mug. "You got that right. Got a question for you, Dottie. Is Mabel rich?"

Dottie sat down. "She's comfortable but not what you'd call wealthy."

Rick looked at Virginia. "What about Harriet?"

"She's always complainin' about not having enough money."

Rick turned his palms up and shrugged. "So why would anyone want to kidnap them?"

Scarlett sat down in Virginia's armchair, facing Rick. "What other explanation is there? They can't have disappeared into thin air." She drummed her manicured fingernails on the arm rest.

Dottie had a sudden thought. "What if Mabel was mistaken for Virginia? Even though Virginia's younger, they look alike. And they have a similar build."

Everyone stared at her.

"If that's the case, there's your motive," Rick said.

Scarlett nodded. "I'm reluctant to admit it, but I think Rick's right."

Rick frowned. "You say this happened two days ago?"

"Night before last," Virginia said.

"Assuming they've been taken, I'd expect a ransom note or at least a phone call by now. I heard from those sleazebags the afternoon Fred disappeared. "

"The phone rang several times this mornin'," Virginia said. "When I lifted the receiver, the caller hung up."

"Was anyone else around when you told Fred about the money?" Dottie wondered.

"The evening Fred flew in from Rio we went to a local watering hole. We stood around the bar, drinking beer, while I brought Fred up to speed on everything."

"Including the inheritance?"

"Yeah. Something's niggling at me." Rick rubbed his temples. "Can't think straight right now."

Dottie nodded. "I know the feeling."

He picked up his coffee mug and drained it. "What have the police done so far?"

"They're searching the Forest Preserve where Mabel and Harriet were geocachin'. They've checked local hospitals, and Harriet's friends. They're comin' by in the mornin' to give us an update."

"Why don't you tell us exactly what happened after Fred arrived in Savannah," Dottie said.

"There's not a lot to tell." Rick shrugged. "I'd told Fred I was in big trouble and asked him if he could help me out."

An audible sigh escaped Dottie's lips. How many times had she heard that one!

"Let me guess," Scarlett said. "You invested in one of those ponzi schemes. Or you got involved in a shady business deal that went wrong."

Rick glared at Scarlett and Dottie. "You two think you know a lot about me, don't you?"

Virginia flashed them a warning look.

Dottie forced herself to take a deep breath. "I only know what Fred's told me."

Rick's shoulders sagged. "My gambling debts got out of control. I owe a pile of money."

The words leapt out of Dottie's mouth before she could stop them. "How much?"

Virginia's eyes blazed. "That's Rick's business, Dottie!"

Rick pulled himself to the edge of his chair. "The day after Fred arrived in Savannah, some of the River Ghost gang members went to my house while I was out. They took Fred. Figured they'd get me to cough up what I owe." He shrugged. "Trouble is, I don't have that kind of money. And neither does Fred."

"How do you know it was this syndicate that kidnapped Fred?" Dottie asked.

"They phoned me that afternoon and threatened to kill him if I didn't co-operate. When I made it clear I didn't have the money, they tried to get me to steal prescription drugs from the pharmaceutical company I work for."

"I suppose you're going to say you couldn't go through with it," Scarlett said. Her voice oozed with distain.

Rick bristled. "Damn right I couldn't. Why d'ya think I'm lying low?" He grabbed his mug and headed to the kitchen. "I need more coffee."

Virginia lowered her voice. "What's got into you, Scarlett? We don't want him takin' off again."

Rick placed the fresh mug of coffee on the table. He sat down and folded his hands between his knees.

Scarlett tapped her foot on the hardwood floor. "Do you have any idea where Fred's being held?"

"Somewhere on Hilton Head."

Dottie sat up straight. "What makes you so sure?"

"Some of the gang live on the island. I've heard them talk. I know where one of them lives and I've already had that house checked. A lot of big houses in the plantations are surrounded by trees and bushes. It wouldn't be difficult to hide someone. And sometimes owners are away months at a time. An empty house would make an ideal hiding place. I've got friends who've been trying to help. So far, no luck."

"Do you think he's still alive?"

Scarlett's question sent a jolt through Dottie.

Rick rubbed his eyes with fisted hands. "Yesterday I told them I needed proof. They let me talk to him."

Dottie felt her body slacken with relief. "What did he say?"

"Not much. He did say something odd though."

Dottie's heart began to race. "Tell us his exact words."

"He told me he was okay. Then he said, 'Tara it ain't.' That was it. Then they cut him off."

"Tara was the name of the plantation in *Gone with the Wind.*"

"That's the other reason I think he's here on the island. It sounded like he was trying to tell me he's in one of the plantations."

"There's something you need to know." Dottie told Rick about searching his house after she and Mabel arrived in Savannah. "We wanted to find out what was going on."

Rick nodded. "Makes sense."

"We went back the next day to do a more thorough check. While we were upstairs, we heard people walk into the house, and men's voices. We hid in the closet. When we came down later we found a man's body lying behind the sofa. The tip of his left index finger had been cut off."

Rick's face grew pale. "That's the Ghosts' signature."

"The man was wearing a pin-striped suit and red running shoes," Dottie added.

Rick inhaled sharply and rubbed his hands over his face.. "Oh, shit. I could see it coming. Charlie Cranshaw is … was a gang member, but he'd become a liability. Too fond of the booze."

"He dropped off a package at the Hampton Inn with Fred's ring inside," Dottie said.

"He hangs out with a weirdo called Benjamin. He's the one who likely got Charlie to deliver the package."

Scarlett said, "How come you didn't know Charlie had been murdered? It's been all over the news."

Rick sighed. "Haven't seen TV or read a paper for the past week. Haven't been near the house either. I told you I've been keeping a low profile."

"Where've you been staying?"

"With friends."

"I'd like to know why these creeps chose your house to carry out the murder," Scarlett said.

"They've been watching out for me, so they knew the house was empty. Carrying out Charlie's murder in my house was clever. First, the body was unlikely to be discovered for some time; secondly, I'd be the chief suspect."

Dottie frowned. "You seem to know a lot about this River Ghost syndicate."

"Some of 'em played poker at my place. It wasn't until I owed a stack they turned on me."

Dottie needed to clear up one more thing. "Why did you leave a note at the Colonial Cemetery a few days ago?"

Rick raised an eyebrow. "Note?"

"It was in your handwriting."

"What did it say?"

"It was hard to decipher. The rain had blurred some of the letters. It said something about Hilton Head Island and the lighthouse. There was also a time and day—six-thirty p.m on Thursday.

"Go on."

"We went to Harbour Town expecting to meet you."

"Hold on. What were you and Mabel doing at the cemetery?"

"After we'd found Charlie Cranshaw's body, the police questioned us for hours. We thought a ghost tour would help take our minds off things. At Colonial Cemetery Mabel took a picture of a person standing by a gravestone. He was dressed in a white robe and smoking a cigarette. We decided to visit the cemetery in the daylight and found the note under a stone."

"The ghost was about my height. Right?"

"It was you, wasn't it?"

Rick shook his head. "For starters, I don't smoke. Gave it up a year ago. Your ghost is Benjamin, the one I told you about. Everyone knows him around Savannah. He likes to dress up as a ghost and stand around the cemetery at night, smoking. Sometimes he leaves notes."

"How do you explain the handwriting?" Dottie said. "It looks identical to yours."

"No idea." Rick scratched his head. "Wait a minute. Benjamin was at a party in my house a while ago. I found him upstairs in the office rifling through my stuff and kicked him out. Later I noticed my Day-Timer was missing."

"How come I found it in your desk the other day?"

"That's a new one."

Scarlett was puzzled. "Why would he steal your Day-Timer?"

"He's a snitch for the syndicate. They probably wanted to find out what I was up to."

"That doesn't explain why the note's in your handwriting."

"That's the crazy kind of thing Benjamin does."

Rick's writing would be easy to copy with its bold lettering and dramatic flourishes, but Dottie wasn't buying it. "Why would he do that? And why leave a cryptic message in a graveyard instructing the finder to be at a certain place at a certain time?"

Rick ran his hands through his hair. "You'd have to know this guy. He once left flyers at a hotel desk advertising free carriage rides around Savannah and a glass of champagne, in honor of the company's twentieth anniversary. Anyone interested should show up at the marketplace at ten the next morning."

"What happened?"

"About twenty-five people turned up. Benjamin watched from behind a tree in the square."

Dottie thought back to Harbour Town. She remembered seeing a man loitering in one of the stores. "What does this Benjamin look like?"

"He's scrawny. Scraggly black hair. Sometimes he has a beard. I've seen him with three different moustaches. Why?"

"I noticed a man who looked like that hanging around one of the stores in Harbour Town. Later, I saw him in the crowd by the harbor, watching two men drag a body from the water. He took a close look at the body as well."

"Sounds like Benjamin. My guess is the River Ghosts wanted him to identify the drowned man."

"So you're saying if he's the one who left the note at the cemetery, he'd want to see if anyone turned up at the lighthouse," Dottie said.

"You got it."

Dottie told Rick about the severed finger. "Is it possible that this Benjamin could have sent the parcel with Fred's watch and the finger?"

"As unlikely as it sounds, I'd say yes. He could have found Fred's watch upstairs in the bedroom. And Fred's journal. Your address would be in there for sure."

Virginia spoke up. "Mabel phoned to tell me about the body. She and Dottie thought it might be you. I was scared, let me tell you."

Rick walked over to Virginia, sat down, and put his arm around her. "I'm not that easy to get rid of, honey."

A tear slid down Virginia's cheek.

Dottie cleared her throat. "Anyway, when the police arrived at the harbor, the man had disappeared."

Rick nodded. "Definitely sounds like Benjamin. Now I remember what was bothering me earlier. I saw him in the bar when Fred and I were having a drink. I bet he was listening in. When he's had a few, he uses another name. Let me think." He stared into the distance, his foot tapping on the floor. Suddenly, his eyes shot wide open. "Bugsy, that's it. After the gangster, Bugsy Siegel.

Chapter Seventeen

Mabel stared at the blank screen.

"Dial 911!" Harriet urged.

"The battery's dead."

Harriet looked at Mabel in disbelief. "Let me see." She took the cell phone from Mabel and pushed the buttons. "How often do you charge it?"

"When it runs out."

Harriet gave an exasperated sigh.

"It's no use worrying about that now. We'll have to go to Plan B."

"We don't have a Plan A yet."

"You're right." Mabel glanced at the bug spray lying on the carpet. She picked up the can. "We could spray bug killer into his eyes as soon as he walks through the door."

"No way! I'm not going through that again."

"It would be easy. I'll hide behind the door and when he comes in, I'll spray him, like this." Mabel pressed the button. Nothing happened. "Empty can. So much for that." Mabel sat down on the bed. "What we need is an escape plan."

"You've got to be kidding! The tower's too high up for us to jump out the window, and the door's always locked."

"We need to work on Bugsy," Mabel said.

"What do you mean?"

"Use reverse psychology."

"Huh?"

"Act as though we've no intention of trying to escape."

"You mean, pretend we're giving up?"

Mabel nodded. "If Bugsy believes we're resigned to our fate, he might let his guard down a bit."

"Then what? We knock him out and tie him up?"

"Don't be silly. Once he's distracted, we look for a chance to escape."

"It sounds far-fetched to me."

"All right. What about this: each time he brings our meals, we don't say anything. If he asks questions, we'll give short responses. Like 'yes' or 'no', that kind of thing."

"He's not very observant. Can't see that working." Harriet paused. "We could try to get him talking about something that interests him."

"Good idea. He's got a tattoo on his forearm," Mabel said. "We could ask him about that."

"Anything's worth a try."

"While he's distracted, one of us will make a run for it," Mabel said. "Have you noticed he doesn't lock the door behind him when he brings the food?"

"What if he catches you?"

Mabel smiled. "So, you've already decided I'll be the one who runs for help."

After a while, Harriet sighed. "Okay, it's worth a try. And I'll be right behind you."

"Let's give the silent treatment a shot first."

***

Around six, the door clicked open. Bugsy strode in with two brown paper bags in his hands. He scowled and placed them on the dressing table. "Here's your dinner."

Neither woman responded.

"It's hamburgers. And I got iced tea."

He glanced over his shoulder. "You two lost your tongues? I ain't got time to play no games." He stormed off, slamming the door so hard a picture fell off the wall.

Mabel looked at Harriet. "Well, so much for Plan A."

Harriet sank onto the nearest bed. "I'm scared, Mabel." Beads of sweat had broken out on her forehead. "Bugsy's a loose cannon. You never know what he'll do next."

Mabel put a comforting arm around Harriet.

Harriet sniffed. "He's in a foul mood. If we've been kidnapped so he can blackmail Virginia and Scarlett, maybe things aren't going well with the negotiations."

Mabel shuddered. "That's what I'm afraid of."

***

The following morning, Bugsy arrived half an hour early. Gone was the comb-over of greasy hair and the ponytail. His head had been completely shaved, but he still had his moustache. He wore a tan suede jacket, a white shirt and black jeans and reeked of sickly-sweet aftershave.

"I got you a special treat today. Egg McMuffins." He grinned at Mabel as he placed the tray on the dresser. His crooked teeth spoiled the improved image. "There's hash browns, orange juice, muffins and two large coffees. And I got some of them kiwi fruits."

Why so much food, Mabel wondered.

Mabel rapped on the bathroom door. When Harriet opened it, she nodded her head in Bugsy's direction. "He's here, and he's in a good mood."

Moments later, Harriett walked out of the bathroom, wearing the robe that hung behind the bathroom door. She'd wrapped a towel like a turban over her wet hair.

She walked over to the dresser, opened one of the paper bags and sniffed the contents. "Oh, McDonald's! I love their breakfasts."

You better make the most of it," Bugsy said. "That's all you get till tonight, so it's gotta last."

"You're all dressed up," Mabel ventured.

Bugsy smoothed down his jacket with both hands. He cleared his throat. "I got a big meeting to attend." He took a silver cigar case out of his jacket pocket, removed the cigar and threw the case into the wastebasket.

With a smug grin, he put the cigar in his top pocket. "I gotta feeling I'll be celebrating today."

Encouraged by Bugsy's response, Mabel continued. "Where is the meeting?"

His eyes became slits. "None of your beeswax, lady!"

Harriet looked worried. "Are you going to bring us supper?"

"Depends on how long the meeting lasts." He pulled something out of his jacket pocket. "I forgot to leave these yesterday." Bugsy dropped two packs of Benson & Hedges cigarettes on the dresser and moved to the door. "Here, catch." He tossed Harriet a lighter.

As soon as Bugsy left, Harriet tore open one of the packs and lit a cigarette. She closed her eyes and inhaled. "You have no idea how good this tastes!"

"Harriet, do you realize what this means?"

For a moment, Harriet didn't say anything. Then a smile crossed her face as she looked at the lighter. "The fool has given us a weapon. You were right when you said he wasn't the sharpest knife in the drawer."

Mabel paced the floor. "He'll be gone all day. That gives us plenty of time to come up with Plan B. We may never get a chance like this again, so we'd better not blow it."

As she passed the wastebasket, Mabel spotted the silver cigar tube that Bugsy discarded. She picked it up and looked at the letters on the side. 'H. Upmann.' It was the same cigar brand as the one used to make the fake finger. What an odd coincidence! Or was it? Could Bugsy have made the finger as practical joke and mailed it to Dottie, along with Fred's watch? But why would he do that? She pushed her speculations out of her mind. It was time to think about an escape plan.

They brainstormed for the next few minutes.

"I like your idea of waving a burning pillowcase out the window," Harriet said.

"We need a flagpole," Mabel glanced around the bedroom. "Ah-ah!" She pointed to a side window. "That wooden drapery rail will do."

"Great idea." Harriet climbed onto a cedar chest beneath the window. She lifted off the rail and unhooked a set of flimsy nylon sheers. "Too bad about the sheers. Cotton or linen would have made a good flag."

Mabel tied a pillowcase to the rail and handed it to Harriet. "You're taller than I am, so you should wave it."

They lugged the chest over to the big window. Mabel opened the window and looked out. The leaves rustled as a strong breeze swept through the trees. "It's a bit windy, Harriet. Be careful."

"I will. You light the pillowcase."

"First, we need to make sure there are people around."

They didn't have long to wait. In the distance, a man and a woman appeared on the pathway, pulling a red wagon with two small children in tow. Mabel picked up the lighter, flicked it on, and lit the corner of the pillow case.

Harriet thrust the flagpole through the open window. She began to wave it back and forth, yelling 'Help! Up here! Help us!' at the top of her voice.

The family walked by.

Harriet sighed. "They didn't even glance over."

"The house is too far from the road."

The flames climbed up the pillowcase. A piece of material broke off and a sudden gust of wind hurled the burning missile through the air. It landed on Harriet's outstretched arm. She cried out, dropped the pole and lost her balance. Arms flailing, she fell backward and landed on Mabel.

The two of them lay in a heap on the bedroom floor.

"We must look a right pair of wallys!" Mabel said.

"Wallys? What's that?"

Mabel struggled to sit up. "Fools. Are you okay.?"

She examined her arm. "I've got a small burn, nothing serious."

The two women struggled to their feet.

Harriet glanced at the window. "What about the flag?"

They climbed on the chest. Mabel's heart sank as she gazed down at the charred remains of the pillowcase lying on the driveway. The two women moved away from the window and sat on the edge of Mabel's bed.

Mabel propped up her chin with her hand. "We'd better come up with a good reason why a curtain rod with a half burned pillow case is lying on the ground beneath our window." She stood up. "I'm going to get an orange juice. Want one?"

"No thanks. I need a smoke." Harriet fumbled in her pocket and retrieved the cigarette pack. She lit a cigarette and took a deep draw. Eyes closed, she blew out the smoke slowly. "What time is it?"

"Four o'clock."

"What time do you think Bugsy will get back?"

Mabel shrugged. "Six, seven, who knows?"

They both jumped when a key jiggled in the lock. "He's back early!" Harriet cried.

The door opened. A hulking brown-skinned man with dreadlocks sidled into the room.

Harriet screamed.

He looked at the two women, eyes like steel. "You're coming with me," he wheezed.

Mabel struggled to speak. "Where's Bugsy?"

"He overstepped the mark."

A shudder ran down Mabel's spine. "What do you mean?"

The man drew his index finger across his throat.

"Who are you?" she managed to say.

He pulled a gun from his jeans pocket and pointed it at them. "Get moving."

Chapter Eighteen

Harriet stared at the big man, the cigarette dangling between her fingers. Mabel took the smoldering stub and squashed it out on the saucer that served as an ashtray. She tried to help the frightened woman onto her feet, but Harriet's legs gave way and she fell to the floor.

Mabel shook her gently by the shoulders.

Harriet blinked several times. "What happened?" She trembled as she looked at the man again. "Who's he? Where's Bugsy?"

"I don't know, but we have to do what he says."

A sudden coughing attack overcame the man, and he began to wheeze and gasp for breath. Eyes watering, he fumbled in a back pocket and produced a puffer. After he'd inhaled two short blasts, his breathing settled and the coughing stopped. The gun never wavered.

Harriet used her elbows to push herself into a seated position. With Mabel's help, she stood up.

The man waved the gun at them. "Let's go."

They left the room and walked down the stairs, along a hallway and out the front door. They were halfway down the rain-slicked iron steps when Harriet clutched her stomach and bent forward.

Mabel caught up to her. "What's wrong?"

"I'm going to be sick."

"What's going on?" The steps shook as the man clumped down behind them.

"My friend's not well."

"Move it!" He pushed Harriet and she almost lost her footing.

Mabel took her by the hand. "Take a few deep breaths."

At the bottom of the steps, the man pointed the gun toward a black SUV with dark tinted windows idling on the driveway. "Get in the back."

A man with a clean-shaven head and a diamond stud in his ear sat in the driver's seat. He glanced around as the women climbed in. Mabel felt a jolt of fear when she recognized the AK 47 with its curved magazine lying in the space between the front seats.

The driver grumbled, "What the hell, Rasta. Lucas don't like to be kept waitin'."

"Lucas doesn't count any more, Stud."

Mabel froze. Was this the same Rasta who'd been threatening Rick?

Rasta squeezed into the back seat beside Harriet. She screamed. He slapped her on the mouth. Harriet heaved and threw up on his lap.

"What the fuck." Rasta grabbed a jacket that lay next to the AK-47 and leapt out of the car.

"Where're you going?" Stud yelled.

Mabel found some tissues in her pocket and wiped Harriet's face. The sour smell pervaded the car.

"Shit!" Stud said and rolled down all the windows.

Mabel glanced out and saw Rasta wiping his jeans with the jacket.

"That's my jacket you cleaning up puke with!" Stud shouted.

Rasta gave him the finger and threw the jacket away.

Stud muttered under his breath.

Back in the car, Rasta blindfolded Harriet. She began to whimper. He secured her hands behind her back with tape. He got out of the car, walked to the other side and climbed in beside Mabel. When he placed the blindfold over her eyes, Mabel felt everything close in. Don't panic, breathe normally, she told herself. She heard a zipping noise and felt the sticky surface of tape as he bound her hands.

He got into the front passenger seat. "Do something to get rid of the smell."

"I've opened all the windows," Stud snapped. "And I don't have no air freshener."

Tires crunched on loose gravel as the car moved forward. A few minutes later, Stud slammed on the brakes then made a sharp right, throwing Mabel against Harriet's shoulders. The two women pitched from side to side at every turn of the winding road.

A siren sounded in the distance. It grew louder. Was it the police? Mabel's spirits soared. Were they about to be rescued? Her hopes were dashed as the siren's wailing faded away.

The car halted. From the hum of heavy traffic, Mabel figured they must be waiting at the lights leading onto William Hilton Parkway, the island's main thoroughfare. If a car pulled up beside them, maybe the driver would see two women with blindfolds on, take the license number and call the police. Then Mabel remembered the car had tinted windows. No one could see inside.

The car pulled away and curved to the right. About twenty minutes later it slowed down and turned left. After lurching along a bumpy road for a few minutes, the car stopped.

Rasta opened the door and ordered Mabel and Harriet out of the car. "I'll take her." He grabbed Mabel's arm.

"Thanks. Leave me with the puker," Stud said. "Let's move them in quick."

Rasta shoved Mabel forwards. "Let's go."

As she moved along, Mabel felt pieces of stone digging into the soles of her moccasins. She tripped over what felt like a tree root and pain shot through her arm as Rasta dragged her to her feet.

Close by, a dog barked. She could hear the other two shuffling behind her.

Rasta pulled her to a stop and a key jiggled in a door. "Okay, lady. Inside."

When Mabel stepped into the building, the smell of stale bacon grease almost made her gag. Rasta sat her down and removed the blindfold. She squinted against the light. Her skin stung as he pulled the duct tape off her wrists. "Any messin' about and the tape goes back on."

Mabel rubbed her wrists to get the circulation moving again. The driver pushed Harriet on to the sofa next to Mabel and removed the blindfold. Harriet cried out when he ripped off the duct tape.

She grabbed Mabel's arm. "What's going on?"

Mabel shrugged. The men exchanged a few hasty words, but spoke in low voices so Mabel couldn't hear what they said. Stud left the house.

When her eyes had adjusted to the dimly-lit interior, Mabel took a good look around. In front of the lumpy sofa sat a coffee table cluttered with paper plates and empty take-away pizza boxes. On her left, two torn armchairs had been placed in front of a large flat screen TV. A kitchen area consisting of a fridge, a small stove and a sink full of dirty dishes was to her right. Flies buzzed over the sink.

In the centre of the room, a single low wattage bulb hung from the ceiling above a battered card table surrounded by plastic chairs. A swarthy-looking man with black hair sat in one of the chairs, smoking. His cut-away vest revealed beefy arms covered in tattoos.

Rasta walked over to the man and spoke to him, his voice almost a whisper. Mabel strained to listen and heard him say, *Lock them in the bedroom,* followed by some garbled words.

As he headed out the door, Rasta spun around. "No screw-ups, Lucas. "

Eyes flashing, Lucas shouted something back in a foreign language. He turned to Mabel and Harriet and snapped, "Okay, you two, come."

They followed Lucas down a short dark hallway. "Welcome to the Ritz," he sneered and shoved them into a small room with two cots. A bulb hung from the ceiling on a shredded cord. Minimal daylight came through a tiny window, high on the wall.

He shut the door. A key turned in the lock.

Harriet sank onto one of the cots. Mabel picked up the musty-smelling blanket from the cot and placed it around her friend's shoulders. Overcome with exhaustion and fear, Mabel began to tremble. She took the blanket from the second cot and pulled it tightly around herself. Instinct told her these people wouldn't hesitate to kill them if they tried to get away. Bugsy had been scary, but these people had a cold-blooded ruthlessness about them.

Mabel glanced around the bleak surroundings. The only other piece of furniture was a badly scratched chest of drawers and a small wooden chair. The paint on the walls was peeling and the faded grey carpet was stained and covered in dust balls.

Where was the bathroom? she wondered.

The ceiling light caught something silver lying in the corner. She picked the item up and found herself staring at an expensive looking fountain pen. Pushing her purple-winged glasses back on her nose, Mabel moved under the light bulb to take a closer look. The brand name *Parker* was engraved on the nib. As she replaced the cap, she saw the words *Industria Brasileira* imprinted on the clip.

The pen was made in Brazil. *Fred Fortune works in Rio. Could it belong to him? Had he been kept in this room?* If so, this could mean that she and Harriet were being held by the gang that captured Fred. Mabel felt the blood drain from her face. A few days ago, they had killed the man in the red shoes. Today, she was sure they had murdered Bugsy, one of their own. Would she and Harriet be their next victims?

Chapter Nineteen

Rick stood up. "Gotta go. If I hear anything, I'll be in touch."

Scarlett watched him leave and stifled a yawn. "I'm off to bed. It's been a long day."

The front door clicked open then closed again. Footsteps pounded in the hallway and Rick strode back into the living room. He handed a torn piece of paper to Virginia. "Found this sticking out from under the doormat."

Virginia unfolded the paper. Her eyes darted over the page. "Oh, no!"

Scarlett snatched the paper out of Virginia's hand, read it and handed it to Dottie. "It's a ransom note."

Dottie's heart raced as she read the words aloud:

"I have the two wimmen. If you want to see them again, you have to pay a randsome. Follow these instruction. Bring 100 thou in small bills in a envelop to Aunt Chiladas parking lot at midnite Monday. DO NOT CALL THE COPS. If you bring the law, youll be sorry.

Virginia's eyes grew wide. "Monday. That's tomorrow!"

"What took them so long to get in touch?" Scarlett said.

Virginia looked at her sister. "I bet those hang-ups yesterday were him."

"Aunt Chilada's is a bar?" Dottie said as she passed Rick the note.

Rick nodded while he scrutinized the note. "It's been around forever. Looks like this has been written by a kid."

Scarlett's red curls bounced as she shook her head. "I think it's someone who wants us to think he's not very bright."

"Why?" Rick said.

Scarlett shrugged. "To keep his identity secret, I suppose."

Rick sat down. "Don't assume there's only one person involved. There could be two or more. It could be a hoax, but we have to take it seriously. "

Dottie nodded. "We sure do. It's the only lead we have."

Virginia added, "Dottie's right. I'll get the money tomorrow morning."

Rick leaned forward. "Something I have to say to you all. This could get out of hand rapidly. You need to let the cops know."

Scarlett's eyes flashed. "Didn't you read what this low life said? No police."

"They know how to handle these situations."

"No," Virginia said. "It's too risky."

Dottie added, "I agree. If this guy or guys are unstable and they get a whiff of the police, who knows what they might do to Mabel and Harriet."

Rick stood up. "Have it your way. I'll see you all tomorrow night around eleven. Virginia, call my cell if anything comes up."

Scarlett looked at Rick. "You're planning to come with us?"

"You think I'm letting the three of you do this on your own?"

"We don't need you. We're perfectly capable!"

"Believe me, Scarlett, I know how these scumbugs operate. It can get nasty, and if more than one of them show up, it'll be even more dangerous."

Virginia glared at her sister. "You heard Rick. You'll follow us in your car, right?" Virginia said.

"No. I'll go on ahead. By the time you arrive, I'll be hidden nearby."

"I feel much better knowing you'll be there," Virginia said.

"I wish I felt the same way. This could all blow up in our faces."

Scarlett frowned. "What are you saying, Rick?"

"That we may end up dead."

Chapter Twenty

Early next morning, after a futile attempt to eat breakfast, Scarlett and Virginia drove to the bank. Virginia took a battered briefcase with her. Since Sergeant Cooper had told them he would drop by with an update sometime before noon, Dottie stayed behind.

He arrived shortly after Scarlett and Virginia left. Dottie invited him into the living room. "Virginia and Scarlett are out, but I'll pass on any information you give me. Would you like coffee?"

"No thanks." Sergeant Cooper sat down. "There's not much to tell. We've questioned the occupants of houses in Sea Pines to see if they noticed anything unusual that night."

"Like what?"

"Anyone walking outside after dark. Strange cars. Nothing came of that. Now we're checking empty houses. We'll call when we have anything to report." He paused. "If anyone gets in contact, call the police immediately. There's the possibility that they may have been abducted."

Dottie cleared her throat. "What makes you think that?"

"It's only a theory right now, but we're not ruling anything out." The sergeant spoke slowly and with great emphasis. "Let me repeat. If you hear from anyone, call this number."

He handed Dottie a business card identical to the one he'd given her a few days ago. "Don't take matters into your own hands. It could be very dangerous. I've seen it happen. People think they can handle things themselves, and they end up getting killed."

"I understand, Sergeant."

After he'd left, Dottie's mind was in turmoil. If they went ahead with their plan, they'd be risking their own lives as well as Mabel and Harriet's.

An hour later, the sisters returned home. Dottie was in the kitchen. "I've made a fresh pot of coffee."

"After the morning we've had I need a caffeine fix." Scarlett poured one for herself and added a sweetener. "We had to hit all four of Virginia's banks."

Virginia put down her briefcase, picked up a mug decorated with roosters and filled it with coffee. "I like to spread my money around. We got the cash. That's the important thing."

"Let's go into the living room," Dottie said.

They plunked themselves down on the sofa.

Scarlett sipped her coffee. "Did Sergeant Cooper turn up?"

"He sure did." Dottie outlined the sergeant's words.

"Phew! It certainly hits home, doesn't it?" Scarlett said.

Dottie nodded. "It's made me stop and think. I'm leaning towards telling the police."

"I hear what you're saying," Virginia said, "but if the kidnapper sees the police, I'm scared he'll kill Mabel and Harriet. I say we give him the money as planned."

Dottie frowned. "Don't forget what Rick said. There could be more than one kidnapper."

"All the more reason why Rick should be nearby," Virginia said.

"I think Virginia's right. I say stick with our plan." Scarlett looked at Dottie. "You're wavering, aren't you?"

Dottie looked at each of them in turn. "I'd feel better if we went over the whole plan with Rick. He's knows much more about these things than we do."

"That's an excellent idea," Virginia said. "I'll call him." She picked up her cell. A few minutes later she got off the phone, "Rick'll be here around ten-thirty tonight.

That'll give him time to hear us out and see if the plan has any holes in it."

"Let's go over everything now so we'll be ready for him," Dottie said.

"I'll start," Virginia said. "At midnight, this blackmailer, whoever he is, will walk over to my car and demand the money. Presumably Mabel and Harriet will be in his car."

"They'd better be," Scarlett replied. "We won't be handing over a hundred thousand dollars unless we can actually see them."

"I suppose he'll want to count the money first."

"That could be awkward," Scarlett said. "It'll be dark."

Dottie added, "He'll probably get into his own car to do that, but we won't let him drive off until Mabel and Harriet are released." They brainstormed for a while, and spent the rest of the day trying to keep their minds occupied with TV, card games and Scrabble.

Rick showed up at ten-thirty as planned. He listened to what they had to say and nodded. "You've covered all the bases."

He looked at each of them in turn, his face serious. "Are you sure you want to do this? It's very risky."

"We're willing to take the risk," Dottie said.

Rick shrugged his shoulders in resignation. "Okay. Remember I'll be nearby." He pulled a gun out of his pocket. "And I've got this, as an added precaution."

Rick left around eleven-fifteen to give himself time to find an unobtrusive parking spot near the entrance. At eleven-thirty, Dottie climbed into the passenger seat beside Scarlett. Virginia sat in the back, clutching the briefcase with her good hand. On their way to the restaurant, Dottie went over the plan in her head one more time. She felt more confident now Rick had given the green light.

They drew near Aunt Chilada's. Dottie peered out the window but there were no cars parked nearby. "I wonder where Rick's got to?"

"He's probably casing the joint, or whatever they call it," Virginia said.

Scarlett huffed. "He's supposed to be looking out for us and he's nowhere in sight."

"Calm down," Virginia said. "You're like a cat on a hot tin roof."

As Scarlett signaled to turn into the restaurant's parking lot, a car drew up about twenty yards away. It was partly hidden by a canopy of trees that overhung the pathway and curbside. The driver flashed his lights.

"There he is!" Virginia said.

Scarlett turned into the empty lot and backed into the nearest corner. She switched off the engine and checked her watch. "It's ten to twelve."

Dottie resisted the temptation to light a cigarillo, knowing Scarlett didn't like the smell. She stared into the dark and waited. Her heart began to race as the minutes went by. At midnight, she took several deep breaths and willed herself to stay calm. Scarlett sat very still, her eyes focused on the entrance to the bar.

At ten past twelve, a car turned into the lot.

Scarlett leaned forward. "Here he comes!"

Dottie strained to get a glimpse of the driver, but the car had tinted windows. He backed the car into a space near the end of the parking lot.

"Why's he parking so far away?" Virginia said.

Scarlett drummed her fingers on the steering wheel. "He's switched off the engine. Good. Give me the money, Virginia."

Virginia handed her sister the large, fat envelope.

Dottie glanced at the entrance. Rick had moved forward, ready to block the exit if necessary.

Five minutes passed. Something's not right, Dottie thought.

The sudden roar of the other car's engine made everyone jump. Lights blazed. Windows were opened and music blared out. As the car drove by, Dottie caught a glimpse of the driver, a girl with spiky orange hair and a cigarette hanging from her lips. Two young males with shaved heads sat in the back seat. They yelled something unintelligible through the window. The car raced out of the parking lot and with squealing tires, turned onto the main street.

"Can you believe it! Here we are, waiting for some dumbass to arrive, and the only car to show up is full of teens," Scarlett muttered.

"I bet they were smokin' pot," Virginia said.

They settled back to wait. A few cars drove by. One slowed down as it passed the bar but drove on. At 12:40, Virginia said, "I don't think this guy is going to show up. Maybe he saw the cars and got spooked."

"You're right. We should go." Scarlett turned on the engine, eased forward and pulled onto the main road. Rick's car moved up behind them.

Dottie felt as though she'd been holding her breath for the last hour. On the way home, she did some breathing exercises to release the tension. They didn't work.

Virginia sighed. "I keep thinking about Mabel and Harriet. They must be going through hell. It's been four days already."

"Mabel's level headed," Dottie said. "She's probably working on an escape plan." She looked over her shoulder at Virginia. "What about Harriet?"

"Harriet's a nervous Nellie."

Scarlett pulled into Virginia's driveway and the three women climbed out of the car. Rick parked behind them, got out of his car, and joined them.

"I wonder what happened," Scarlett said.

"Maybe he chickened out," Virginia said. "What do you think, Rick?"

He stifled a yawn. "No idea. I'm wiped. Let's talk in the morning."

Virginia said, "It's late. Stay over, Rick."

"I think I will."

Chapter Twenty-One

Dottie woke early. At the bottom of the stairs she met Rick creeping out of Virginia's room. "Mornin', Rick."

"Mornin', Dottie," he said, with a sheepish grin. "Sleep well?"

"Not really. I'll put the coffee on."

Once it had brewed, the others wandered in. They helped themselves and sat at the kitchen table.

No one felt like eating much, but Virginia insisted they have some toast or cereal. "It's not good to drink caffeine on an empty stomach."

"Last night was a real fiasco," Scarlett said between bites of toast.

Virginia sighed. "I've been thinkin' we should tell the police."

"What! You were gung ho on not telling them yesterday," Scarlett said.

Virginia sipped her coffee. "I know but to tell the truth, I felt scared sittin' there waitin'."

"I agree," Dottie said. "We can't go through that again."

Rick put down his mug. "The police will go ballistic when they find out you tried to go it alone."

They finished breakfast in silence.

Dottie picked up the coffee pot. "Anyone want more?"

"You can top mine up," Virginia said.

Scarlet pushed her chair away from the table. "None for me, thanks. I'll see if the paper's arrived."

She returned with a manila envelope in her hand. "This was squished between the screen and front door. It's got my name in big letters on the front."

They all watched in silence as Scarlett undid the metal fastener and pulled out a piece of paper. "It's another ransom note."

Everyone crowded around Scarlett to read over her shoulder.

The message was printed in large red letters:

YOUR SISTER, VIRGINIA, AND HER NEIGHBOR HAVE BEEN KIDNAPPED. THEY WILL COME TO NO HARM AS LONG AS YOU FOLLOW OUR INSTRUCTIONS.

WE WILL BE IN TOUCH WITH YOU AT TWO P.M. TODAY. DO NOT CONTACT THE POLICE. IF YOU DO, YOU WILL NOT SEE EITHER OF THEM AGAIN.

RG

Scarlett turned to Dottie. "You were right. They think they've captured Virginia."

"What's going on?" Virginia said. "First, we get that note telling us to go to Aunt Chilada's. Now we get another one."

"They're from different people," Rick said.

Dottie agreed. "The other note was amateurish. There's something very chilling about this one. And it's signed RG. That's for River Ghosts, I assume."

Rick looked at the women, his eyes full of concern. "That's right. This is the group that kidnapped Fred. Now we know for sure they've got Mabel and Harriet as well."

Chapter Twenty-Two

Mabel heard the clatter of pots. Soon, the greasy smell of fried food began to seep into the room. The door rattled open and Lucas shuffled in, a cigarette hanging from the side of his mouth. In his beefy hands, he carried two plates heaped with French fries soaked in gravy with bits of sausage stuck in it. A bulging plastic bag hung over his arm. He placed everything on the cot next to Harriet, who sat motionless, with the blanket still wrapped around her slumped shoulders.

"We need a washroom," Mabel said. As Lucas walked passed Mabel, the odor of stale sweat almost made her throw up.

Lucas jerked his head toward the door. "This way." Harriet jumped at the sound of his voice.

"Come on, Harriet," Mabel said.

Lucas led them to a small windowless bathroom and switched on the light. He nodded to Mabel. "You first."

Mabel wrinkled her nose at the foul smell. Bad drains. She unzipped her capris and tried not to look too closely at the stained toilet bowl. Inside a bathroom cabinet she found a scrap of soap but nothing else of use; not even a nail file. She washed her hands and dried them down the side of her pants.

As she turned to leave, Mabel caught a glimpse of herself in the cracked mirror above the sink. Her face had taken on a jaundiced pallor. The creases around her eyes seemed to have multiplied. Her hair, always difficult to manage, looked like dried yellow stalks pointing in different directions.

She rinsed her face, dried it with her shirt sleeve and opened the bathroom door. "Your turn, Harriet."

Once they'd finished, Lucas escorted them back. He took a deep draw on his cigarette. "Don't get too comfortable. We're leaving tonight."

Mabel's breath caught in her throat. "Where are we going?"

Ignoring the question, he left the room and locked the door.

Harriet burst into tears. "I can't take much more!"

"Pull yourself together. Getting hysterical won't help."

Harriet rooted for a tissue in her jacket pocket and blew her nose. After a few more sniffles, she looked up. "I'm okay now."

Inside the plastic bag, Mabel found four cans of Coca Cola. She took one out and peered at the food. The mound of French fries looked worse now that the gravy had congealed. An image of the kitchen area with its pile of dirty dishes and buzzing flies flashed through Mabel's head.

Harriet screwed up her face. "We can't eat this."

"We've got to eat something. Goodness knows the next time we'll be fed."

Harriet picked up a fork, speared a French fry and bit off the end.

Mabel stabbed a forkful of the unsavory mess. The combination of lukewarm gravy and fries made her stomach churn. She washed it down with several swigs of Coke.

While they picked at the food, Mabel told Harriet about the pen she'd found earlier.

Harriet's eyes grew wide. "You think Fred's been in this room?"

"The fountain pen's from Brazil, and we know Fred's been working in Rio."

"Seems a bit of a stretch." Harriet looked at Mabel. "What do these people want with us?"

Mabel shrugged. "I wish I knew."

"Kidnapping usually involves money," Harriet said. "Maybe they think we're rich."

After another forkful of the fries, Mabel ran the back of her hand across her mouth. "That's all the food I can stomach." She drained the can of Coke.

They fell silent for a few minutes.

Harriet sighed. "My Duke must be frantic with worry. Dottie and Virginia as well. "

Mabel felt her throat tighten at the mention of Dottie. "I'm sure the police are searching. It's only a matter of time before they find us."

Harriet's eyes glimmered with hope. "You really think so?"

"I do. Right now, we should try to get some sleep."

Harriet stretched out and tucked the blanket around her. A few minutes later, Mabel heard gentle snoring.

Mabel lay on the cot and closed her eyes. Her mind wandered back to the two yoga classes she'd taken at the local Y. The stretching and twisting exercises weren't her cup of tea but she enjoyed the relaxation part at the end.

The instructor had encouraged her students to visualize waves lapping on a beach, but Mabel found it far more relaxing to think about driving her red Lotus Elise sports car. She took long breaths and exhaled slowly. As the tension began to melt away, she floated off and dreamt of speeding down winding country roads, brakes squealing around the bends.

Chapter Twenty-Three

A loud bang woke Mabel out of a deep sleep. Heart pounding, she pushed herself into a sitting position. "What was that?"

Harriet was already sitting up, her eyes wide with alarm. "It sounded like a gunshot!"

"It's probably a car back firing." Mabel heard raised voices through the thin bedroom wall. "Sounds like Lucas has company." She strained to listen. "It's no use. I can't make out what they're saying."

Harriet walked over to the far wall and knelt on the floor. She leaned sideways so that her ear was pressed against it. After a few minutes, she groaned and straightened up. "My legs are killing me."

She massaged them. "That's better."

"Well?"

"The only voice I recognized was Lucas's. He sounded very scared." She looked at Mabel. "They're talking about drugs. Someone said 'bathtub crank.' That's slang for poor quality crystal meth. And 'brown crystal.'"

"What's that?"

"Heroin."

"How do you know all this?"

"Years ago I volunteered at a drug rehab for youth in Atlanta. You learn fast."

A man's voice cried out, "Don't shoot!"

Another loud bang pierced the air, followed by a thud. Everything became quiet. After a few moments, Mabel heard muffled voices and heavy footsteps. A door slammed shut.

Both women put their ears to the wall. Nothing stirred in the room next door. The only sound Mabel heard was the distant bark of a dog.

They moved away from the wall and sat on a cot. "If they shot Lucas we could be locked in here for days," Harriet said. "No one knows where we are."

"Not true. Rasta does."

The tiny bedroom window was open a few inches. It was too high for Mabel, so she pulled a cot over to the wall and stood on it. With the extra height, she could see outside. In the moonlight, she spotted a parked truck about ten yards away. Three men were unloading plastic containers from the back of the truck. They carried them toward the house.

Mabel heard muffled voices. Within seconds, she caught the unmistakable whiff of gasoline followed by a whooshing sound. Flames flickered across the window. "Oh my God! The house is on fire." She jumped off the cot and rushed to the door. "Get over here, Harriet. We've got to break this door down."

Harriet ran over. They gave the door a hard push with their shoulders. It didn't budge. "Let's try again, give it all we've got," Mabel said. "Ready? One, two, three!"

They threw their weight against the door. It creaked but didn't open.

Sweat trickled down Mabel's back. "We'll have to kick it down."

They kicked as hard as they could, but Harriet's canvas beach shoes had little impact. Mabel's leather moccasins weren't much better.

Mabel glanced back at the window. Smoke curled through the small opening. She grabbed the small chair at the corner of the room. Using it as battering ram, the two women ran at the door. Two of the chair legs broke.

"It's no use, we're trapped!" Harriet cried.

"We've got to keep trying. Okay, let's give it another go. Ready? Go!" They threw themselves at the door. This time, they felt it give a little. "We're nearly there. One more time!" The door flew open and they tumbled headlong onto the floor.

Mabel's left arm and shoulder took the brunt of her weight. She scrambled to her feet, grabbed Harriet's arm and pulled her up. "We have to get out!"

"Not so fast, ladies!"

Mabel's heart sank when she recognized Rasta's wheezy voice. He loomed in the hallway. Stud stood next to him, smirking at the two women. Mabel cried out as Rasta seized her by the left arm, but he didn't ease his grip. Stud grabbed Harriet.

They were halfway across the living room when Mabel saw the body. Her breath caught in her throat. Lucas lay spread-eagled on the floor, his undershirt drenched in blood. His eyes stared at the ceiling and his mouth drooped hideously to one side. She glanced at Harriet whose face had turned a sickly grey.

The two women were hustled outside, into the back of the black SUV. Rasta jumped into the passenger seat. Flames from the burning house leapt into the night sky and thick smoke billowed out of open windows. As the vehicle pulled away, Mabel saw the walls cave in.

Chapter Twenty-Four

"Gun it!" Rasta yelled.

"Chill out, man," Stud said. "It's a fire, not a drug raid."

"Odds are someone saw the perps set fire to the house and called the cops."

"Why should we worry? It wasn't us who done it."

Rasta thumped his fist on the armrest. "Get moving."

Their words caught Mabel by surprise. If they weren't involved in the fire, who was responsible?

As though reading her thoughts, Stud said, "It'll be the Dunes brothers. They've been out to get him since Lucas double-crossed them over that bathtub crank."

Stud flicked his cigarette out the window and accelerated down the laneway in a swirl of dust. As the car bumped along, Mabel tried to take in as many landmarks as she could, certain that Rasta would blindfold them once they were closer to their destination. Harriet sat with her face in her hands. She'd be no help.

They passed several mobile homes on either side of the lane, one with a pit bull chained to the fence. The car slowed down and turned onto a poorly lit paved road. Mabel struggled to find a landmark such as a bank or a restaurant but realized it wasn't likely as they were driving through a residential area of prefabs, trailers and the occasional bungalow.

After a while, Rasta pointed. "Take that side road."

Stud turned onto a dirt lane and parked on the grass verge. Rasta climbed into the back seat, blindfolded Mabel and Harriet, stuck tape over their mouths and taped their hands behind them.

Soon after they got back on the paved road, Mabel heard sirens. When the wailing grew louder, Stud pulled over. "Here come the cops and fire engines. They won't find nothin' left. Everythin'll be burnt to a crisp by now. Including Lucas."

"Shut it," Rasta said.

"I didn't mean nothing by it, man."

"You seem to have forgotten our little talk."

When the sirens faded, Stud pulled back onto the road.

Mabel's arm began to throb. She tried to block the pain by trying to figure out where they were heading. She knew they were driving along a paved road but that didn't tell her much. Her mind wandered to last month's European vacation. By the time she'd relived the dangerous adventures she and Dottie had faced, she felt quite exhausted.

A while later, the car turned onto another road. Within minutes it slowed down, turned left onto gravel and stopped. Rasta opened the back door. Mabel winced as he grabbed her left elbow and pulled her out of the car. The door slammed shut.

She heard another door open and close. Feet crunched behind her.

"There's no need to dig your hands into my back," Harriet said.

Rasta shoved Mabel forward. After she'd taken a few steps, a door in front of her clicked open. "Get in the house," Rasta said. Inside, Mabel breathed in the smell of citrus. She could feel the hard surface of a tiled floor through the thin soles of her moccasins.

Rasta pushed her onto a cushioned seat and removed the tape and blindfold. As she waited for Harriet, Mabel rubbed her sore arm. She glanced around. She was sitting on a leather sofa surrounded by fancy cushions of various shapes and sizes. Across the room, a crystal chandelier hung over a large dining room table with high-backed chairs. Not my cup of tea, Mabel decided, but much better than their last digs. A lump formed in her throat as she thought how Dottie would love this room. Seconds later, Stud walked in with Harriet. As soon as he removed the blindfold and tape, Harriet dropped onto the sofa next to Mabel.

"All right, you two. Upstairs." Rasta pointed to the staircase, visible through the open doorway.

The two women pulled themselves off the couch, crossed the hallway and climbed up the winding staircase, with Rasta close behind. Mabel jumped when a grandfather clock in the hallway began to chime. She checked her watch. Eleven o'clock.

When they reached the landing, Rasta unlocked and opened a door opposite the stairway. He switched on a light and cocked his head at the two women. "In there." He followed them inside.

Mabel swallowed hard. "What are you going to do with us?"

Rasta looked at her with unflinching eyes. "As long as we get what we ask for, you'll live." He left and locked the door. When the key turned, Mabel's legs began to shake.

Harriet sat down on one of the beds, her face in her hands.

Mabel walked to the window. In the moonlight, the black SUV was clearly visible. Neatly clipped bushes lined the gravel driveway and she could just make out the road beyond. She'd hoped to get some sense of where the road led but heavy foliage blocked her view. As her eyes swept over the SUV again, Mabel spotted the first few letters of the license plate.

She turned to Harriet. "I need a pencil and piece of paper."

Harriet pulled her hands away from her face. "What for?"

"To write down part of the SUV's license plate."

Harriet found a pen and paper in a bedside table and handed them to Mabel. Mabel jotted down the letters. "It's too bad I can't see the whole thing, but even a few letters or numbers can help the police trace a vehicle."

Mabel tucked the paper into her purse. She looked at Harriet. "I think Rasta's contacted Virginia about a ransom."

"What makes you think that?"

"Something he said. 'As long as we get what we ask for, you'll live.'"

"What if Virginia refuses to give them the money?"

"That's not going to happen." Mabel hoped she sounded more confident than she felt. She glanced around the room. It reminded her of the place in Sea Pines, except this one was decorated in various shades of blue. Pictures of sailboats, canoes, and ocean liners dominated the walls. In the far corner, an open door revealed an ensuite bathroom. At least they could shower and wouldn't have to request bathroom break.

Harriet pointed to the mini fridge near a coffee table. "What's with the fridge? Seems strange to have one in the bedroom of a private home."

"The owners probably enjoy snacking before they go to bed." Mabel smiled. "Maybe there's a bottle of champagne inside."

"How can you be so flippant! We're being held hostage by cold-blooded criminals who could kill us at any time!"

"I'm trying to be positive." Mabel heard a noise in the corridor outside their room. "What was that?"

"It sounded like glass shattering."

Low voices came from the hallway. The two women strained to listen. Mabel picked out "... *that was no accident,"* then *"Fred better not try that again."* Some muffled words followed. Then, *"... start putting more pressure on his brother."*

The words faded as feet clomped down the stairs.

Mabel turned to Harriet. "Did you hear that? Fred's name was mentioned."

In the room next door, footsteps padded across an uncarpeted floor. A door slammed. A few minutes later a toilet flushed. The two women looked at each other.

"That could be him in the next room," Harriet said.

"If so, let's hope it's the right Fred."

Harriet frowned. "How can we find out?"

"Don't know at this moment, but we'll work on it."

"Then what?"

"Escape and tell the police."

"Dream on!"

"Someone might get careless and—"

Harriet cut in. "leave the bedroom door open? Yeah, that's likely to happen!"

Mabel ignored Harriet's pessimism. "First, we need to know where we are," she said. "Before we were blindfolded, I noticed a few things."

"Like what?"

"The neighborhood we drove through was poor. You know, prefabs, trailers, that kind of thing."

"Go on."

"Then we were blindfolded. We got back on the paved road and after a few minutes the traffic got heavier. We drove about ten minutes and then turned right. The car stopped briefly and I heard a woman's voice. She said something about Shipyard Road."

Harriet's face lit up. "That's the main road into the Shipyard plantation! I play bridge there every two weeks with a group of friends. Good for you for paying attention. I guess I was too upset to notice anything."

"Don't be hard on yourself. The main thing is we know which plantation we're in. And that's a big step forward." Mabel glanced at her watch. "It's almost midnight. We need to get some sleep but, we're both wired." She opened the fridge door. Inside, she found bottles of vodka and gin, along with orange juice, tonic water and soft drinks. She took out the gin bottle and held it up.

Harriet smiled for the first time in days. "What's with these people? That other place had brandy. This one has vodka and gin."

"Why don't you have a bath. It'll help you unwind," Mabel said. "Then we'll have a drink."

Harriet hesitated.

"It worked at the other house."

"You're right." Harriet disappeared into the bathroom.

Mabel decided to search the room. By the time Harriet appeared, wrapped in a navy bath towel, Mabel had accumulated a corkscrew bottle opener, an extension cord and a small hammer. The hammer puzzled her. Maybe the owner had used it to knock in nails when he or she hung the pictures.

"That feels better! Now I'm ready for that drink," Harriet said.

Mabel was pleased to see Harriet in better spirits. She poured gin into crystal glasses and added tonic water. "Too bad we don't have any lemon."

"Can you believe they use crystal glasses in their bedroom?" Harriet said. "That's classy." She raised her glass. "Here's to a quick rescue."

"I don't want to burst your bubble, Harriet. But even if we could get in touch with the police, we can't tell them for certain where the house is located."

Harriet said nothing.

As they sipped their drinks, Mabel decided their only option was to come up with an escape plan. Or find a phone. And the odds of that were next to zero.

**

Moonlight poured through the window. Mabel and Harriet didn't want to sleep in darkness so they'd decided not to close the drapes. As Mabel lay in bed, her mind raced. How could they find out who was in the room next door? Was it Fred Fortune? Could they somehow get a message to him? Or could they trick their captors into telling them? Fat chance! With a frustrated sigh, Mabel rolled over.

A flash of light from a passing vehicle beamed through the bedroom window. It illuminated a picture of *The Titanic* on the facing wall. Those poor souls must have felt so desperate, so alone. Even SOS messages didn't save them.

Mabel sat up in bed. She'd learned some basic Morse code years ago as a Girl Guide. If she could tap out an SOS on the wall, would this person—Fred?—recognize it? Maybe, if he'd been a Boy Scout in his youth. She'd use the hammer she'd found earlier.

Mabel glanced at Harriet, who lay on her back, mouth open, fast asleep. Someone could be in the corridor keeping watch. Mabel strained to listen for sounds outside the bedroom door but nothing stirred. She moved over to the wall and made three staccato taps with the hammer, followed by three well-spaced ones. She ended with three more quick taps.

The minutes ticked by. Nothing. Maybe's he's a heavy sleeper. Then, footsteps slapped across the floor in the room next door, getting louder as they approached the wall. Mabel tapped out another SOS message. Three taps emanated from the other side.

Boots clunked on the stairs and stopped outside her bedroom. Heart racing, Mabel rushed across the room, leapt into bed and pulled the duvet over her head. A slight clicking sound came from the door. Mabel peeked over the duvet. In the moonlight, she saw the brass door knob begin to turn.

Chapter Twenty-Five

Mabel froze as the doorknob jiggled to the left then right. After one more turn it stopped. Footsteps faded away and feet clomped down the stairs. She blew out a long sigh of relief, climbed out of bed and listened at the door. Muffled voices floated up from the living room.

She tiptoed back to the wall and tapped out another message. This time, no one responded.

***

The following morning, Mabel woke to the sound of a running shower. A few minutes later, Harriet walked out of the bathroom in a black cotton robe. "Found this behind the door." She rubbed her hair with a towel. "You look like you're in pain."

Mabel massaged her forehead. "My head's throbbing."

"Rough night?"

Mabel told Harriet about her harrowing experience.

"You should have woken me up."

"Why? You couldn't have done anything."

Harriet stopped drying her hair. "The guy next door… do you think it's Dottie's Fred?"

"Could be. I'll try again later." Mabel stood up. "I'm going to take a shower too. I wish we had a change of clothes."

"I'll see what I can find."

Mabel popped two Advil she found in the medicine cabinet. After a long hot shower, she wrapped herself in a large bath towel. By the time she came out of the bathroom, her headache had almost disappeared.

"What do you think?"

Mabel looked at Harriet in amazement. She was dressed in a French Maid's outfit, complete with a frilly white apron and cap, and black fishnet stockings. Mabel suppressed the urge to giggle. "Where on earth did you find that?

"At least it's a change of clothes." Harriet pointed to one of the closets. "You're not going to believe it. It's full of party outfits. Go take a look."

Mabel's eyes darted over the assortment of togas, princess dresses, and witch's outfits. "Whoever lives here must own a costume business or a party supply store." She glanced back at Harriet. "Couldn't you find any regular clothes?"

"Loads of them but they're a size 4. And as for underwear, all I could find were these." Harriet held up a handful of black lacy thongs.

"I think I'll stick with my cotton knickers."

"We can wash our clothes in the bathroom sink, and wear the costumes while they're drying," Harriet said.

At the far end of the closet, Mabel spotted something bright yellow. It was a banana costume of all things. She tried it on. Although baggy, it felt comfortable. "This will do." She pulled on the hat as well.

The two women grinned at each other. "Whoever delivers breakfast is in for a surprise," Harriet said.

"Or a heart attack."

A while later, a key turned in the lock. Stud sauntered in carrying two paper bags and placed them on the dresser. Dark stubble covered his chin and his eyes were bloodshot. When he glanced at the two women, his mouth fell open. One of the bags dropped from his hand. He lunged to grab it mid-air, but missed. "Shit," he muttered as the bag split and coffee spilled over the floor. He left the room and locked the door.

"Did you see the look on his face?" Harriet said.

Mabel laughed. "He was gobsmacked."

The spilled coffee smelled good. Mabel picked up the empty cup. She took the other cup out of the bag, removed the lid and carefully poured some of the hot liquid into the empty one. She handed it to Harriet.

They added cream and sugar and drank their coffee in silence.

Harriet bit into a donut. "So, let's get back to our next door neighbor. Can you do your name in Morse Code?"

Mabel stared at her. "Of course! That's it. I'll tap out my name. If it's Fred Fortune, he'll know who I am. Good thinking, Harriet!"

"You've met him?"

"No. But Dottie's told him about me."

"Duke taught me some Morse Code years ago. I may be able to figure out the message."

"Great! If he taps anything out, can you write down the dits and dahs? Let's give it a try."

A loud clatter next door caught their attention. Feet pounded across the floor. Mabel put down her coffee cup and rushed over to the wall. She listened. Everything fell quiet in the adjoining room. Harriet retrieved the notebook and pencil and joined Mabel.

Mabel tapped out her name and, for a few seconds, nothing happened. Then a light tap, tap, tap from the other side. Harriet scrambled to write down the message.

Once the tapping stopped, Harriet sorted out the letters. "The third letter's clear. It's a single dit, which is E." Her eyes narrowed as she took a closer look. "Okay, got it! The first and second letters are F and R."

"That has to be Fred."

Harriet turned to Mabel. "Can you do 'Dottie?'"

"I think so."

"Start tapping. If it's Fred Fortune, he'll realize we know who he is." Mabel had almost finished tapping DOTTIE when the door rattled. She hid the hammer under a nearby armchair, and Harriet shoved the notebook into the bedside table drawer. The door opened. Rasta and Stud strode in. Without saying a word, they hustled Mabel and Harriet out of the room and down the corridor. Mabel demanded that Rasta tell them what was going on. He ignored her. When they reached the last door, he opened it, flicked on a light switch and pushed the two women inside. The door clicked shut and the key turned in the lock.

"What's that all about?" Harriet said.

"Maybe they heard us tapping."

Harriet gave an exasperated sigh. "Just when we were getting somewhere."

Mabel looked around. The room was decorated in bright reds, blues and yellows. A giant stuffed panda sat at the head of one twin bed and a giraffe on the other.

"No prizes for guessing the occupants of this room," Harriet said.

"Look at this," Mabel said. She walked over to a kid-sized desk. On the top sat a laptop computer.

"Oh my God! Does it work?" When Harriet pressed the ON key, a soft whirring sound came out of the laptop. Seconds later, the screen came on. "I'll send an email to Dottie and Virginia! And my Duke!"

"Be quick," Mabel urged. "Once they find out there's a laptop in this room it'll be too late."

A minute later, Harriet banged the desk with her hand. "Damn! It isn't connected to the internet. It's only set up for kids' games."

Mabel's heart sank. For a few moments it looked as though they'd hit pay dirt, as her hubby, Alf, would have said.

"Kids have their own phones these days," Harriet said. "We should take a look around. With a bit of luck, maybe we'll find one."

Mabel remembered a friend's cell phone had disappeared when he stayed with friends who had young children. It had turned up in a toy box. "Let's start with that pile." She pointed to the far corner of the room.

By the time they'd finished, cars, dolls, and stuffed animals lay strewn over the bedroom floor.

"Now what?" Harriet said.

Out of the corner of her eye, Mabel saw a flickering light. She dashed over to a red plastic dump truck. Inside it lay a bright blue cell phone. Images flitted across the screen. Mabel held it up to show Harriet. "Look at this!"

"Call Dottie's cell!"

What was the number? Mabel's mind had gone blank. She closed her eyes and concentrated.

"Hurry!"

"Just a minute... Ah, got it." She took a deep breath and punched in the number. After four rings it went to voicemail. Mabel tapped her foot as she listened to Dottie's long-winded greeting. Finally, it was over. 'We're being held in a house." She spoke in an urgent voice. "We think it's in Shipyard Plantation. Fred Fortune is..."She turned to Harriet. "The phone's gone dead. We need a charger."

They checked the desk drawers, closets and bookshelves and even looked under the beds.

"Not to worry," Harriet said. "You left a message, that's the important thing. We'll be rescued soon."

Mabel put the phone back in the truck. "Let's hope."

The morning dragged on. Harriet found a game of Monopoly in the closet. They tried to play but couldn't concentrate.

Harriet stood by the window and watched for the police.

"It could be a long wait."

"So?" Harriet said. "I haven't anything better to do."

"I'm not happy with the message I left," Mabel said.

"Why?"

"I didn't have time to say anything about the house we're in."

"What could you have said?"

"That it has a paved driveway, for a start. And that it's about half a mile from the turn-off, things like that."

Harriet turned away from the window. "It might be another day before they find us."

Or more, Mabel thought. And what if Dottie doesn't get the message? "We should be looking for opportunities to escape."

The door flew open. Rasta stormed in and threw paper bags on the dresser. "Be ready to leave in fifteen minutes." He sounded out of breath, as though he'd been running.

Harriet's voice trembled. "Where are we going?"

He didn't reply.

Mabel fisted her hands. "We have a right to know."

Rasta swung around. He picked up a chair and slammed it onto the hardwood floor. The chair split in two. "You have no rights, lady. Understand?"

Suddenly, he began to wheeze. His face turned red and he clutched his chest. Gasping for breath, he sank to the floor.

"He's having an asthma attack!" Mabel grabbed Harriet's arm. "Quick, now's our chance!"

As Rasta struggled with his puffer, Mabel whacked it out of his hand and rushed passed him. The two women dashed down the stairs to the front door. By some miracle it wasn't locked. The banana costume slapped against Mabel's legs as they flew down the driveway, turned onto the road, and ran, not daring to look back.

Chapter Twenty-Six

Scarlett placed the ransom note on the kitchen table. They all sat down.

Dottie lit a cigarillo and turned to Rick. "Tell me more about this River Ghosts gang."

Rick ran his hands through his hair. "They're big-time drug dealers headed up by a thug called Rasta."

Dottie blew a ribbon of smoke from the side of her mouth. "And you got involved with them through gambling?"

"Yes." Rick stared into space. "I've been a damn fool."

Scarlett tapped her fingers on the kitchen table. "The note says they'll be in touch at two p.m. today. We've got over four hours to kill. I think I'll go to my room and read for a while."

Dottie wandered into her bedroom, picked up an old magazine that lay on the dresser and half-heartedly glanced through it. A Time Warner Communications ad caught her eye.

With a jolt, Dottie remembered that with all the hoopla over the ransom note, she'd forgotten to check her cell. She had two messages. The first was an ad. The second was from Mabel. When she heard the familiar voice, Dottie dashed into the living room. "I've got a message from Mabel! Where's Scarlett?"

Scarlett rushed downstairs. "What's going on?"

"I've had a message from Mabel."

Dottie replayed it, and put it on speaker phone so they could all listen.

"What time did she call?" Scarlett asked.

Dottie checked. "Just after nine this morning. I must have been in the bathroom when it came through. Now we know where they're being held. And Mabel mentioned Fred at the end of the call. I wonder why."

Rick scratched his head. "We don't know which house. They could be anywhere. It's a big plantation."

"Can you replay Mabel's message and turn up the volume?" Virginia said. "We may have missed something."

They listened to the replay.

"I didn't pick up anything new," Scarlett said.

The others agreed.

Virginia said, "You could check the last number called and leave Mabel a message telling her we need to know more about the location of the house."

Dottie said, "A great idea as long as she's able to recharge the phone." She left a message on Mabel's cell.

"We have to tell the police what's going on," Scarlett said. "They'll check the cell number Mabel called from and find out who it's registered to."

Dottie nodded.

Virginia lit a cigarette and inhaled deeply. "They'd have to do a house-to-house search. A lot of these homes are left unoccupied months at a time, so it'll be a long haul."

Rick held up his hands. "Hold it."

The three women looked at him.

"You can forget about telling the cops. Once these sleazebags find out someone's on to them, they won't hesitate to kill."

Scarlett said, "That's not what you said when we were planning to hand over the money to the kidnapper. You were gung ho about telling the police."

"That's because I had visions of you getting shot by some trigger-happy nuthead. I've got a better idea than bringing in the police. Now that we know which plantation, I've got friends who can do some… er… some surveillance for us."

"Now you're talkin', Virginia said.

Scarlett frowned. "If the police use unmarked cars, how would they know?"

"These people can sniff cops miles away."

Dottie was puzzled. "Why would your friends be better at surveillance than the police?"

"They're experts at this kind of thing. Trust me."

"Trust you? That's a good one, Rick," Scarlett said.

Virginia glared at her sister. "Cut it out, Scarlett. We need to concentrate on the rescue. "

Dottie stubbed out her cigarillo. "If your friends find out which house they're in, then what?"

"We bring in the police."

"How long will this take?" Scarlett asked.

"Hard to say. But these guys know where to look. And what questions to ask."

Dottie sighed. "I don't like it, but I guess it's our best option for now."

"Maybe Mabel will phone again and give us more information about the location," Virginia said.

Rick turned to leave. "I'll get onto my guys. Virginia, call me as soon as you hear anything."

***

The day dragged on. Between TV and card games, the women strategized a plan of action. They decided that, when the phone rang, Dottie would answer while Scarlett listened in on the kitchen extension and took notes. Dottie's apprehension grew. What if the kidnappers' demands were out of reach?

Doubts about Rick lingered. Could he be involved in Mabel and Harriet's kidnapping? Was it possible he'd made a deal with the kidnappers that if Virginia paid the ransom his debt would be cleared?

Dottie sat on the edge of the sofa by the phone on the coffee table. Scarlett positioned herself at the kitchen table, phone, notepad and pen ready. The clock struck two.

A couple of minutes passed. When the phone rang, Dottie jumped. Her heart raced as she picked it up. It was a recorded message, urging the homeowner to vote in the upcoming midterm elections. Dottie took a deep breath. Stay calm, don't lose your nerve. They waited for another hour. Still no call. Scarlett made a fresh pot of coffee.

"There's a lemon loaf that Judy next door brought over," Virginia said. "You might as well serve it with the coffee."

"None for me, thanks," Dottie said.

Scarlett shook her head. "I'm too wound up to eat." She carried the tray with mugs and one slice of lemon cake for Virginia.

"I'll give Rick a call," Virginia said and punched in his number on her cell. After a few seconds, she left a short message. "Rick, we haven't heard from these people. Now what?" She hit the END button and lit a cigarette.

"He's probably busy with those friends of his," Dottie said. She was beginning to have doubts about the so-called friends. Were they really checking around the plantation, as Rick had said. Or was it a ruse?

Virginia looked worried. "He shoulda phoned by now. I got a bad feelin'." She took a long drag.

"That's nothing new where Rick's concerned." Scarlett said.

Virginia's eyes sparked. "I'm tired of your sarcastic comments, Scarlett. If you've nothing good to say, shut up!"

Scarlett looked sheepish. "Sorry, Ginny."

Virginia flicked her cigarette ash into the ashtray. Her voice dropped. "Somethin's not right. I can feel it in my bones."

Chapter Twenty-Seven

Mabel's legs felt like lead. She paused to catch her breath. Across the road, two young boys on bikes stopped and stared. Behind her, a pathetic cry pierced the air. She turned around to find her companion sprawled on the sidewalk, hands outstretched. "I can't go any further."

Mabel pulled Harriet to her feet. "We've got to keep moving before they catch up to us."

As though on cue, Mabel heard the hum of a car engine. She breathed a sigh of relief when a silver Lexus appeared around the bend. She leapt into the road, arms flailing. Harriet rushed over and joined her.

The car screeched to a halt. Two beady eyes peered over the steering wheel.

"Let's get in," Mabel said.

They rushed to the back door. Mabel tried the handle but it wouldn't budge. She hammered on the window. The driver looked at her, his face a mixture of confusion and alarm. Mabel brought her hands together and put on her best 'please help' expression. It worked. The back door popped open and the two women scrambled in.

"This is an emergency!" Mabel said, between shallow breaths. "Please drive us to the nearest police station."

The man turned around. His elfin face was dominated by a fleshy pock-marked nose. His tiny moustache twitched. "What for?"

"We were kidnapped," Mabel said. "We've just escaped."

"Ha! That's a good one!" He popped a candy into his mouth.

"It's the truth."

He scrunched up the candy paper and threw it out the car window. "So where's the costume party?"

Mabel gritted her teeth. "We've got to get hold of the police. Any minute now the kidnappers will catch up." She paused. "Look. I know this all seems far-fetched, but you've got to believe us. These people are murderers. And they're armed."

The man's face grew serious. "I don't know where the sheriff's office is."

"Have you got a cell phone?"

"No. My daughter Mandy does though. She lives in California."

Harriet screeched. "This is an emergency! We need to get in touch with police. Now!"

"Wait! I just remembered something." The man opened the console door and pulled out a bright pink cell phone. "Here you are. Mandy left it behind when she flew back to L.A. yesterday."

Mabel grabbed the cell and punched in 911. After giving the operator her name, Mabel told her about the kidnapping. "We escaped about half an hour ago. We're sitting in back of a car we managed to flag down. We're afraid the kidnappers will catch up to us."

The operator's brisk voice rang out. "Where are you now?"

Mabel looked at the driver. "Where are we?"

"On Shipyard Road."

"Shipyard Plantation!" Harriet yelled.

Mabel passed on this information. "Let me talk to the driver," the operator instructed.

Mabel handed him the phone.

In a firm but calm voice, the operator asked for his name.

"Chester Bottomly."

She told him to drive to the security gate.

Bottomly handed the phone to Mabel. "Don't worry. You'll soon be safe and sound. Seat belts on. Get ready for the ride of your life!"

Mabel and Harriet struggled to buckle up as the car sped forward.

Mabel placed the phone to her ear. "I'm back. Any more instructions?"

"Is Mr. Bottomly heading to the gate?"

"Yes."

"Good. Leave the phone on. And tell him to lock the car doors."

Mabel passed the message on. Without taking his eyes off the road, Bottomly pressed the door lock button.

As they got closer, she began to breathe more easily. Seconds later, she heard the roar of an engine and turned to see a black SUV racing toward them.

"The kidnappers are right behind us!"

Unlike Harriet, Mabel's costume was so big she couldn't duck down.

Bottomly glanced back. A huge grin appeared on his face. "They won't catch me!" He hit the gas pedal and the car swerved toward a live oak at the side of the road. Mabel braced herself for the impact.

Bottomly managed to get the Lexus under control but it was too late. The SUV drew up alongside them. Rasta sat in the passenger seat next to Stud. His lips curled into a sneer as Stud slammed his car into the side of the Lexus.

"Dickhead!" Bottomly shouted. He put his foot down to the floor and headed to the security gate where two police cars were waiting. Mabel looked back. The SUV had spun around and disappeared in a cloud of dust.

Bottomly had almost reached the gate when a large black dog ran in front of the car. "Godammit!" Bottomly yelled and slammed on the brakes. Heart pounding, Mabel gripped the back of the passenger seat as the car veered off the road, bumped over a grassy embankment and plunged into a lagoon.

Mabel's seat belt tightened from the sudden jolt when the car hit the water. It sank a few feet, landed on the bottom of the shallow lagoon and listed to the right.

Bottomly unlocked all the doors. "Can you two get out?"

Harriet managed to open her door about an inch. "The door's stuck."

Bottomly stuck his head out of the window and peered behind. "Something's blocking it – looks like a tree branch." He climbed out of the car into the water and grabbed the algae-covered obstacle. It wouldn't budge.

Mabel wriggled over to help Harriet. They pushed hard. Mabel moaned as a searing pain shot through her arm.

"What's wrong?" Harriet said.

"It's my arm."

"Sit back. Okay, Mr. Bottomly, we can do this. Are you ready? One, two, three!" Harriet leaned against Mabel and pushed the door with her feet, while Bottomly tugged at the branch. He almost fell over when it gave way but managed to stay upright. Harriet scrambled out of the car, stepped into the lagoon and pushed the dead branch out of the way.

Mabel tried to climb out, but her costume got stuck on the seat belt. She grabbed the material with both hands and tugged hard. The costume tore away with such force that she tumbled backward out of the car into the muddy water.

Soaked to the skin, with green algae stuck on the rubbery costume, she struggled to her feet only to discover she was face to face with an alligator. It lay in the water about five yards ahead of her. Its yellow eyes were just above the water as it moved toward her.

Chapter Twenty-Eight

A cracking sound echoed through the lagoon. Mabel swung around. Bottomly stood at the side of the car, aiming a rifle at the alligator.

"Almost gotcha!" He grinned at Mabel. "Don't you worry, little lady. That critter's days are numbered!"

Several police officers appeared at the top of the hill. "Drop the gun!" one yelled. "Now."

Bottomly glanced up in the direction of the voice.

He hesitated for a few moments, then threw the gun toward the embankment. The policemen ran down the grassy slope. One picked up the gun and two raced over to Bottomly.

Another policeman helped Harriet to the side of the lagoon. He returned for Mabel and introduced himself as Deputy Sheriff Carroll. He held Mabel's arm. As they squelched through mud toward the embankment, the alligator closed its jaws, turned and swam away. "Are you all right, Ma'am? That 'gator got close."

"I feel a bit shaky, but I'll be fine. Did you catch the kidnappers?"

"We're on to them. We'll need statements from all of you."

"There's someone else to worry about, Sheriff. His name is Fred Fortune," Mabel said.

"Who's Fred Fortune?"

"We think he was being held captive in the room next to ours."

Deputy Carroll looked puzzled. "Another kidnapping? First I've heard of it."

He took a phone out of his pocket. While the deputy made his call, Mabel kicked herself for mentioning Fred. Why hadn't she stopped to think before opening her mouth? The gang had threatened to kill him if the police were called in, and now they'd be out in force.

The deputy finished his call. "No kidnappings have been reported, other than yours." His eyebrows furrowed. "You sure about this?"

Mabel nodded.

After he'd guided Mabel to the edge of the lagoon, the deputy said, "When you and Mrs. Milloy make your statements, try to think of anything that might help. About the house where you were held captive, or about the kidnappers themselves. The sooner we start looking the better chance we have of capturing them, and finding this Fred Fortune."

She watched the police escort Bottomly up the embankment. "I hope poor Mr. Bottomly doesn't get into trouble. He rescued us from the kidnappers. And he scared away that alligator."

"Shooting alligators is against the law, Ma'am. They're an endangered species." The policeman smiled. "Under the circumstances I doubt he'll be charged."

Harriet joined them.

"You two stay here. I'll be right back."

Once he left, Harriet said, "Are you all right, Mabel? If an alligator came that close to me, I don't know what I would do. You were very brave to stand your ground."

Mabel assured her bravery had nothing to do with it. "When it began to swim toward me, I froze...." Let's talk about something else."

"We're finally free!" Harriet smiled. "I can't wait to see my Duke's face when he knows we're safe."

"The police want to question us first."

"I suppose that'll take hours."

Mabel remembered the statements she and Dottie were obliged to give after they'd discovered the body in

Rick's house. "Deputy Carroll told me they'll drive us home afterwards."

"Let's hope they rescue Fred and capture Rasta and Stud and the rest of those creeps soon," Harriet said.

Mabel nodded. "Everything happened so fast in the end....I feel sorry for Mr. Bottomly."

"I don't. He nearly got us killed."

"Think about it. There he was, minding his own business, when two crazy women dressed as a banana and a French maid leap into the road begging him to let them into his car."

"No wonder he looked alarmed."

"And he got us away from Rasta and Stud. Even though we ended up in a lagoon."

Harriet nodded. "You're right. And if he hadn't fired his gun at the alligator, who knows what might have happened."

Mabel shuddered. "I don't want to think about it."

"Of course you don't." Harriet sighed. "I can't wait to sleep in my own bed. And have Duke fuss over me. He makes the best shrimp and grits. How about you, Mabel?"

"Right now, I need to take off these muddy shoes, get out of this costume, or what's left of it, and take a long hot bath," Mabel smiled. "And see Dottie again."

Chapter Twenty-Nine

Dottie carried the tray of empty mugs into the kitchen and filled the sink with hot soapy water. When the phone rang, her stomach clenched. Was it the kidnappers?

After a slight pause, Virginia cried, "Heavens to Betsy! Thank you! We'll be waitin'!"

Virginia's voice quivered as she hung up the phone. "You're not goin' to believe it. That was the deputy sheriff. Mabel and Harriet are free!"

Tears rolled down Virginia's cheeks. She plucked a tissue from the box in front of her and dabbed her eyes. "The deputy sheriff's drivin' them here right now."

A wave of relief poured over Dottie. All the waiting and worrying was over. She dried her hands and joined Virginia and Scarlett in the living room.

Blinking back tears, Scarlett and Dottie smiled at each other.

Virginia wiped a hand across her eyes. "I better let Rick know." She reached for the phone, punched in his number and waited. Her foot tapped on the hardwood floor. A few seconds later, the tapping stopped. A frown creased her forehead as she left a message asking him to call.

"Ginny, you know that bottle of champagne that's been in your fridge ever since I got here?" Scarlett said. "How about we break it open when they arrive?"

Virginia's eyebrows shot up. "Now you're talkin'! Go get the champagne flutes. And Dottie, would you heat up some appetizers? I'll keep a look out for Mabel and Harriet."

As Dottie busied herself in the kitchen, she wondered why Rick hadn't answered his phone.

Five minutes later, Virginia called out. "They're here!" Before the two women had climbed out of the cruiser, everyone rushed outside to greet them.

They climbed out of the car, Harriet, still in her French maid costume and Mabel in a mangled banana costume with bits of green slime stuck to it.

Virginia whooped with delight and gave Mabel a one-armed hug.

Scarlett laughed as she bear-hugged Harriet. "What's with the French Maid outfit?"

"It's a long story," Harriet said.

Dottie grabbed Mabel's hands. "That's the last time you go geocaching when I'm around."

"Okay, everyone, let's go inside," Scarlett said. "It's time to celebrate."

"What's that green stuff all over you, Mabel?" Virginia said.

"Algae. I fell into a lagoon."

Outside the front door, the two women removed their mud-caked shoes and placed them on the doormat.

Scarlett searched the hall closet and produced an assortment of footwear. "Try these." She handed Mabel a pair of bunny slippers.

Harriet found an old pair of mules.

"Why don't the two of you go have a shower first," Virginia said. "There are plenty of towels in the bathroom cupboard. Then pop into my bedroom. You'll find all kinds of tops and sweatpants in my closet."

Mabel smiled. "Thanks, Virginia. A shower would be great. And I can't wait to get out of this outfit."

Harriet said, "I'll wait until Duke gets here. He'll have a good laugh when he sees me dressed like this."

Mabel slipped into Virginia's room. She reappeared a short while later in purple velour sweat pants and an orange top, brushing her damp hair. She joined Virginia and Harriet in the living room. "That feels much better."

Harriet kept glancing through the front window. "Where has my Duke got to?"

"I'm sure he'll be here soon," Virginia said. "Come have some champagne."

While Dottie served the appetizers, Scarlett handed out flutes of bubbly and proposed a toast. "To Mabel and Harriet's safe return."

Everyone raised their glasses.

Virginia took a sip and set down her glass. "Now, we want to know everything that's happened the last five days."

Scarlett gave her sister a dirty look. "Really, Ginny. The poor women must be exhausted."

Harriet shrugged. "I'm flying high right now."

"I'm wired too," Mabel said. "We'll probably collapse in a heap later."

Harriet's eyes opened wide. "Get ready to hear some wild stuff. You won't believe what happened to us."

Apart from oohs and ahs and the occasional gasp, the women sat very still as they listened to Mabel and Harriet's story.

When Mabel mentioned Fred, Dottie broke in. "Are you sure it was Fred in the room next to you?"

"Not at first. But later he tapped out his name in Morse Code. I'd almost finished tapping Dottie's name when we were whisked off to another room."

Dottie's mouth went dry. Would Fred meet the same fate as Bugsy and the red shoe man?

It wasn't until Harriet described how they ran down the street in their costumes that the atmosphere lightened up a bit.

"Two kids were about to get on their bikes when they saw us," Mabel said. "Their eyes were like saucers."

Dottie laughed. "I wish I'd been there with my camera."

"What about Mr. Bottomly?" Virginia chuckled. "It's a wonder he didn't have a heart attack when the two of you ran into the road and waved him down."

"Once he got over the initial shock, I think he saw himself as the hero, rescuing poor damsels in distress," Mabel said.

Her face grew serious. "The thing that's bothering me is why did this hoodlum Bugsy kidnap us?"

"It may be a case of mistaken identity," Dottie said. She explained her theory.

"Of course!" Mabel knocked a fisted hand on her forehead. "Why didn't I think of that? Virginia and I do resemble each other." She glanced at Virginia. "Only you're much younger."

"Rick is sure the ghost in my garden was Bugsy," Virginia said. "He thinks when Bugsy decided to kidnap me, he wasn't sure how to go about it. So he followed me during the day to check out my routine. Then at night, dressed as a ghost, he crept through the garden and spied on me through the window."

Harriet's eyes grew wide. "How creepy is that!"

The front doorbell rang. "I'll go," Scarlett said. Muffled voices could be heard; feet clomped across the hallway. Scarlett walked into the living room, followed by Duke. "Look who's here!"

Harriet rushed over and flung her arms around her husband.

"Thank God you're back," Duke said, kissing her firmly on the lips.

"What happened to you, Duke?" Virginia said. "You look white as a sheet."

"Some idiot slammed into the back of my car on 278. I got a doozy of a fender bender. I would have been back ages ago if it wasn't for the police asking a ton of questions."

"You're here, that's all that matters," Harriet said.

He blinked back tears. "I've missed you, honey. I'm taking you home right now."

As he took a closer look at Harriet, his eyes widened. "What in tarnation are you wearing?"

She smiled. "I'll tell you about it over a cup of hot chocolate." She looked at Virginia. "Thanks for everything. I'll drop by tomorrow. We still have plenty more to talk about."

"You just get on home," Virginia said. "Don't even think about anythin' else right now."

"Let's go, honey." Duke put his arm around Harriet's shoulders and guided her out of the room. The front door opened and closed behind them.

Mabel helped herself to a spring roll and turned to Virginia. "Have you heard from Rick?"

Virginia shook her head. "I left a message." She lit a cigarette. After a quick drag, she placed the cigarette on her ashtray and turned to her guests. "It's almost seven. How about we order pizza? You choose the toppings, Mabel."

Mabel sighed with pleasure. "Sausage, pepperoni, onions, green peppers and mushrooms are my favorites"

"Sounds good. We'll get a meatless one as well," Virginia said. She phoned Giuseppe's. "They've had a rush on. Delivery won't be for another hour," she announced.

"No problem," Scarlett said. "While we're waiting, I'll take drink orders."

Quack! Quack!

Dottie looked up in alarm. "What's that?"

Scarlet rolled her eyes. "It's Ginny's ring tone. I keep telling her to change it but she takes no notice."

As Virginia listened, she gripped the phone so tight her knuckles turned white. She turned to Scarlett. "That was Rick."

Scarlett's eyes grew wide. "What did he say?"

Virginia didn't reply. She sat motionless.

Scarlett walked over to Virginia and touched her shoulder. "Tell me what Rick said, Ginny."

Virginia swallowed hard. "He said, 'They finally caught up with me.' Then the line went dead."

"Does that mean the gang has found Rick?"

"Either that. Or he found them."

Virginia dismissed her words with a wave of her hand. "My head's in a muddle right now." With a deep sigh, she sat back in her chair. "Whatever's goin' on, it's bad."

Chapter Thirty

Virginia picked up her cigarette and tapped ash into the tray. Closing her eyes, she took a long drag and blew the smoke from the side of her mouth. "We need to let the police know about Rick's message."

Scarlett nodded. "I'll phone the sheriff's office."

While she made the call, Dottie cleared away the empty champagne flutes and left-over appetizers.

"They'll get back to us shortly." Scarlett hung up the land line.

No one spoke for a while. Scarlett flipped through a magazine. Virginia stubbed out her cigarette and sat back in the armchair, staring into space.

Mabel rooted in her pocket, retrieved a grubby looking peppermint and popped it into her mouth. "I'm not looking forward to another police interrogation."

When Beethoven's Fifth rang out, the three women looked startled.

Dottie picked her cell phone off the coffee table. It was Flora at the Hampton Inn. "Mrs. Flowers? Another gift has been delivered for you. It's wrapped in cellophane and tied with a red bow."

"Is it perishable?"

"No. It's a book. It's called *Earthen Delights Book Three: Go Nuts: Grow Your Own Almond Tree,*" Flora said.

God, what next? "I'm not sure which day we're coming back but would you keep it for me?"

"Of course."

Dottie switched off the cell and looked at Mabel. "It looks like Ernest has sent another gift. Counting the ornamental cabbages, it's the fourth one." She told Mabel about the pecans and the herbal teas.

"He's smitten."

Dottie rolled her eyes. "He's a pest. He thinks we're still at the hotel. I'd better phone him." She picked up her cell.

"If you ignore him, perhaps he'll take the hint," Mabel said.

"Good point."

At that moment, the landline rang. Scarlett answered and spoke briefly then put down the phone. "The police are coming right over."

***

Dottie recognized the burly figure of Sergeant Cooper as he walked into the living room, accompanied by a female officer, whom he introduced as Corporal Hurley.

Sergeant Cooper got straight to the point. "My officers are waiting outside." He looked at Mabel. "We need you to identify the house. I know this won't be easy but the smallest detail could make a big difference, Mrs. Scattergood."

"Of course."

He retrieved his cell. "I'll let my men know."

Once Mabel had left, the sergeant suggested they sit down. Corporal Hurley stood behind her superior, notebook and pencil in hand.

"Now, let's start from the beginning. Mrs. Makefield, I'll start with you. How do you think Benjamin Smiley—Bugsy—found out about the money?"

"When Rick's brother Fred arrived in Savannah, they went to a local bar," Virginia said. "They hadn't seen each other for a while so they had a lot of catching up to do."

"How do you know this?"

"Rick told me."

"You seem to know Mr. Fortune very well."

"He and I... we're an item."

"Go on."

"Bugsy was in the bar."

Scarlett cut in. "Rick knew about Virginia's money and, being a big mouth, he told Fred. Bugsy must have overheard the conversation."

Virginia's eyes blazed. "Fred's his brother, for heaven's sake, Scarlett. Why wouldn't he tell him?"

The sergeant cleared his throat. "Okay. Let's get back to business." He glanced at each of them in turn. "What happened after Harriet Milloy and Mabel Scattergood were kidnapped?" His eyes narrowed. "Bugsy contacted you, didn't he?"

No one answered at first. Then Virginia spoke up. "Someone did. Two days after it happened, we got a ransom note. It wasn't signed."

"Why weren't the police informed?"

"The note said if we told the police, they'd kill Mabel and Harriet," Dottie said.

"So you decided to take matters into your own hands," the sergeant's eyes pierced Dottie's. "Am I right?"

Dottie glared right back. "What choice did we have?"

"Do you still have the note? I need to see it."

Scarlett stood up. "It's in my room. I'll get it." Moments later, she returned with the paper.

Before he took the note, the sergeant pulled on a pair of plastic gloves "I don't expect anyone thought of wearing gloves to protect any fingerprints that may be on it."

They all shook their heads.

After he read the note he placed it in an envelope, which he handed to Corporal Hurley. "So tell me what happened."

Dottie explained how they'd waited in the restaurant car park until twelve-thirty but no one showed.

"Was Rick Fortune involved?"

"Yes," Dottie said. "He tried to talk us out of it."

Sergeant Cooper slapped his hands on the armrests. Everyone jumped.

"The police are trained to handle these situations. You were lucky the kidnappers didn't show up."

He leaned forward and addressed the three women. "What you did was very dangerous and irresponsible. You're dealing with people who have no compunction about killing."

"We all realize now it was a dumb thing to do," Dottie said.

The sergeant didn't say anything for a few moments. He turned back to Virginia. "Tell me about Fred Fortune's disappearance. Why do you think he was kidnapped?"

"I think this gang—they call themselves the River Ghosts—kidnapped Fred to put pressure on Rick to pay his gambling debt."

The sergeant nodded. "How much does he owe?"

"Half a million." Virginia sighed. "Problem is he doesn't have that kind of money."

The sergeant looked at Scarlett. "You told me on the phone Rick Fortune had disappeared and may have been kidnapped by this River Ghost gang. Why would they bother to do this if he can't give them what they want?' He glanced around. "Any theories?"

After a slight hesitation, Virginia said, "Rick told them he could get the money but needed more time."

"That doesn't explain why they kidnapped him."

Virginia shrugged. "They were probably fed up with waitin'. Figured they'd put some extra pressure on him would be my guess."

"Tell me about this call you got from Rick Fortune today," the sergeant said. "When did he phone?"

"About an hour ago."

"What exactly did he say?"

"They finally caught up to me.' Then he hung up."

"And you took this to mean they've kidnapped him."

"It looks that way."

Sergeant Cooper's brows knotted together. "You're not sure?"

Scarlett broke in. "What my sister's trying to say—
"

"Let Mrs. Makefield answer the question."

Virginia cleared her throat. "I believe that's what he meant, yes."

He stood up and looked at each of the women in turn. "From now on, make sure you keep me informed of everything that happens. Is that clear?"

They murmured their assent.

The corporal pocketed her pencil and notebook and the two of them left.

"Whew! He didn't pull any punches," Scarlett said.

"He's right about the risks we took," Dottie said. "Anything could have happened."

Shortly after the police departed, the pizza arrived. Scarlett paid the delivery man and placed the boxes on the kitchen table. When she opened one of them, a cheesy, oniony aroma filled the air. No one felt like eating. Dottie suggested they put the pizzas in the fridge for now and heat them up later.

"I wonder if the police are getting anywhere with their search for the house," Scarlett mused.

As soon as the words were out of her mouth, the phone rang.

Virginia looked at Dottie. "Would you mind gettin' that?"

Dottie picked up the phone. Her heart sank as she listened to Sergeant Cooper's words. She hung up the phone and looked at the three women. "They found the house but it was too late."

"What do you mean, too late?" Virginia's voice rose to a high pitch.

"Sorry. I didn't mean to alarm you," Dottie said. "The house was empty. It was obvious they'd left in a rush."

"I expected that," Virginia sighed. "How will they ever find Fred and Rick now?"

"They won't get far," Dottie said. "The police will already be on the lookout for the SUV."

"I'm going for a walk to stretch my legs," Scarlett said. "Do you want to come, Dottie?"

"I'll stay with Virginia."

"Don't be fussin' over me," Virgina protested. "You go with Scarlett."

Dottie had made up her mind. "I'm staying put."

Just after Scarlett left, the front door clicked open. "I'm back!" Mabel called out. "I can smell pizza! I'm going to grab a slice and some milk."

Dishes clattered. Within a few minutes, Mabel carried a tray into the living room and placed it on the coffee table. She sat down on the sofa, picked up the pepperoni-smothered pizza slice, and bit into it. "This is good."

Virginia looked at Mabel. "So how did it go?"

"Not well. We found the house much faster than I'd imagined. It's amazing how much you take in even when you're blindfolded."

"Didn't you see it when you were escapin'?"

"The only thing on our minds was to get away as quickly as possible. Anyway, I waited in the van while the officers checked out the place. The front door was unlocked, which simplified things. They found dishes in the sink, cigarette cartons and beer bottles but no sign of Fred or Rick."

Dottie felt sick. "I wonder where they've taken them."

Mabel finished the pizza slice, drank the milk and placed the dishes on the tray.

Virginia looked at her, her eyes full of concern. "You must be exhausted. Why don't you have an early night?"

Mabel stifled a yawn. "That sounds like a great idea." She took the tray into the kitchen,

"Leave the dishes," Dottie said. "I'll do them later."

"Thanks." Mabel headed upstairs.

"Let's have a brandy," Virginia said. "It's on the sideboard."

Dottie poured two generous shots into snifters and handed one to Virginia.

Virginia took a long sip. "All kinds of things are goin' through my head right now, and none of them are good."

Dottie put her snifter down. "I'm curious about something you mentioned earlier on."

"What was that?"

"After you'd finished telling us what Rick said to you—that they'd finally caught up to him—you said, 'Maybe.' What did you mean?"

Virginia glanced away. With a long sigh, she turned back to Dottie. "Rick's charmin', great company, and he's good to me. But he's weak. Over the years, he's got himself into so many scrapes. If it hadn't been for Fred rescuing him time and time again, Rick would likely be servin' time right now."

Virginia put down her snifter. "Remember Rick told us this gang wanted him to steal prescription drugs?"

"Which we didn't mention to the police," Dottie said. "Rick said he refused to steal them. In fact, he was adamant about it."

Virginia nodded. "Rick meant what he said. At the time."

"That's what you meant by 'maybe'. You think he may have changed his mind?"

"Yes. What I haven't told you is this gang leader—he goes by the name Rasta—wants Rick to join forces with him."

Dottie inhaled sharply. Things were worse than she'd imagined. "So when you told Sergeant Cooper that the gang believed Rick would find the money—"

"That wasn't true. The River Ghosts know he can't come up with it. That's why they've been after him to steal drugs. I didn't want Sergeant Cooper asking more questions."

Virginia yawned. "I think I'll call it a night. I know it's early but I'm gonna try to get some shuteye." She stood up. "I'm glad we've talked about this, Dottie. It's been preyin' on my mind."

Once Scarlett had returned from her walk, Dottie got ready for bed. Her mind raced as she brushed her teeth. Had Rick agreed to steal the prescription drugs in exchange for Fred's release? If so, they'd hold on to Fred until Rick handed over the drugs.

Could they have taken Fred to another plantation house? Not likely. Perhaps they'd taken him to an abandoned building somewhere. Or one that was under renovation. Dottie remembered reading a thriller where the victim was hidden in such a house.

Ernest might be able to help. He was in the construction business, and many of his projects involved the renovation of old houses. It was a long shot but worth looking into.

Chapter Thirty-One

The following morning Dottie phoned Ernest, hoping to catch him before he left for work. He answered on the first ring. "Dottie! What is going on? Did you get the herbal teas and the book I sent to the hotel? I was beginning to get worried when I didn't hear back from you—"

Dottie cut in. "It's a long story. Right now, I need your help."

"I'll do my best. Go ahead."

"Are houses under renovation sometimes left empty for days or weeks at a time?"

"That is an odd question! It happens quite often. There are lots of reasons for delays, like late deliveries. Sometimes owners have second thoughts about things like bathroom design. Or they may decide to change the floor plan at the last minute. Did I tell you about the guy whose wife couldn't decide what kind of kitchen tile she wanted? First, it was ceramic. Then slate. Finally she chose porcelain. Cripes, it took over three months—"

Dottie cut in. "Do you ever have a problem with squatters?"

"Haven't come across the problem myself but it's not uncommon. Why?"

"The things I'm about to tell you are in strictest confidence, Ernest."

"Of course."

Dottie gave him a brief summary of what had happened over the past week.

"Kidnapping! That's serious. Are you sure?"

"Positive."

"It sounds like the plot from one of those cheap thrillers. You'd be amazed at what some people read—"

"Ernest!"

Ernest cleared his throat. "Sorry. I'll ask around, see if there's any talk of squatters. Most of my properties are in Savannah but I'm in touch with contractors from all over. Leave it with me and I'll get back to you."

***

Two days later, police were still trying to track down Stud's SUV. With no leads on the whereabouts of Fred and Rick, things were looking grim.

Dottie had almost finished her first coffee of the day when Ernest called.

"You won't believe this," he said. "Talk about coincidence."

"I'm listening."

"Just come from a Victorian house I'm renovating here in Savannah. Noticed some large footprints on the attic stairs."

"Wouldn't that be normal?" Dottie said. "There must be all kinds of tradesmen climbing up and down the stairs."

"But we haven't started work inside yet. Anyway, I went upstairs. In the early 1900s it was the maid's quarters. Still has the old-fashioned narrow bed, a chest of drawers and a wooden trunk, all covered in dust and in bad shape. There's a small bathroom just off the bedroom—with an old fashioned sink and one of those clawfoot bathtubs."

"Go on."

He cleared his throat. "I noticed a Styrofoam coffee cup and a McDonalds paper bag in the far corner of the room. I checked the bag. The half-eaten burger and six fries inside looked pretty fresh."

Only Ernest would count the fries.

"So someone's been there recently," Dottie said. "How did the intruder get in?"

"There was no sign of a break in. I checked all the ground floor windows and the back door."

"Who has keys to the house, besides you?"

Ernest paused. "Aside from the owner, I don't know."

"Did you notice anything else?"

"Yes!" Ernest's voice squeaked with excitement. "Next to the cup was a sleeping bag and an open paperback, *Dead in the Water,* one of Stuart Woods' Stone Barrington ex-cop stories. I read it ages ago. I thought there were a few plot flaws—"

"Ernest!"

"Sorry…. Anyway, I checked the bathroom and saw a toothbrush and toothpaste in a Styrofoam cup, a towel and a bar of soap. They'd all been used."

"That's it?"

"It is."

"I'd like to take a look around," Dottie said. "When will you be back at the house?"

"Around three. I'm expecting that delivery I told you about."

"When can I drop by?"

"Let's see. I'll be a while with the delivery people. Might as well say four." He gave her the address and directions.

"Thanks." Dottie rolled her eyes as she pressed the END button. Ernest would have gabbed for another hour if she'd let him.

"Hello!"

Dottie swung around. Mabel stood in the kitchen doorway in an orange and lime green dressing gown and the bunny slippers.

A rush of affection swept through Dottie. "Did you sleep well?"

"A solid nine hours for the third night running."

"It's probably a reaction to all the stress."

"Have you eaten breakfast yet?"

"No." Dottie picked up the coffee pot. "I've been on the phone with Ernest. Remember, I phoned him a few days ago and asked him let me know if he'd heard of any squatters in the neighborhood? Turns out there's one in a house he's renovating." She poured two mugs of coffee. After handing one to Mabel, Dottie told her about the conversation.

"So you're thinking Rasta took Fred to this house? That's a stretch," Mabel said. "It could have been anyone."

"True."

"What about Rick?" Mabel sat down at the table. "You say there was only one sleeping bag."

"According to Virginia, he may not have been kidnapped."

"What?"

"She thinks Rick may be in with the gang."

Mabel's eyes grew wide. "You're kidding."

"That's her theory." Dottie blew out a smoke ring. "Anyway, I've arranged with Ernest to check the attic this afternoon. Why don't you come with me?"

"I will. But right now, my mind's on food." Mabel opened the fridge door. "I think I'll have a couple of pizza slices."

"For breakfast?"

"Waste not, want not," Mabel took out one of the boxes, removed a couple of slices and popped them into the microwave. She took out a bowl of strawberries from the fridge.

"Strawberries?"

"Why not?" Mabel said. "There's loads of them."

Dottie shrugged. "I'll have some fruit and toast myself a waffle."

It didn't take long to prepare breakfast. They'd started to eat when Virginia appeared.

"Good mornin' to you both. I see you found the waffles and strawberries, Dottie." She glanced at Mabel's plate. "Pizza for breakfast? You know, that's not such a bad idea. I think I'll have some." She helped herself to a slice, heated it up and poured a mug of coffee.

Dottie noticed the shadows under Virginia's eyes. "It doesn't look as though you got much sleep."

"I fell asleep around three." She sat down at the table, cradling her mug.

Dottie told Virginia about her chat with Ernest. "Later on today Mabel and I are going to take a look around that house."

"How are you gettin' to Savannah?"

"We'll take the Harley."

Chapter Thirty-Two

They decided to leave for Savannah around three. Dottie headed to her bedroom to get the Harley key from the dresser, but it wasn't there. She searched through the drawers and checked her purse and jacket pockets. She looked under the bed and behind the dresser. Nothing. Two days ago, she'd picked up some painkillers for Virginia. Had she left the key in the ignition?

She joined Virginia and Mabel in the living room and told them about her dilemma. "I know I've been distracted, but I can't believe I'd forget the key."

"Let's go and look," said Mabel.

Ten minutes later, they reached Mary Lou's house and walked around the back. Dottie stopped in her tracks. The bike was gone.

Mabel's eyes widened. "Hell's bells!"

"It must have happened over the last day or so. I'll have to call the Harley-Davidson company right away and let them know the bike's missing. Am I ever glad I took that Theft Waiver!"

They walked back to Virginia's house and told her what happened.

"Who'd do a thing like that?"

Dottie shrugged.

"You can borrow my car to drive to Savannah," Virginia said.

"Won't Scarlett need it?" Mabel asked.

"I'll use Rick's car."

Dottie frowned. "Rick's car is still around?"

Virginia nodded. "He keeps it in his friend, Silas's, garage. While you were out, Silas phoned. He's concerned because the car's been in the garage for three days. Rick uses it almost every day and there's been no sign of him."

Twenty minutes later, after Dottie had finished speaking with the Harley representative, Virginia handed her car keys to Dottie. "I'm not sure I like the idea of you rooting through old attics on your own."

"Don't worry. Ernest will be with us." Not that Ernest would be much use, Dottie thought. On the other hand, if anyone threatened him, he'd probably talk his way out of trouble.

Within minutes, Dottie and Mabel were on their way to Savannah.

As they travelled, Mabel hardly said a word. Dottie glanced at her friend. "What's on your mind?"

"I bet Rick took the bike," Mabel said. "It would be easy to find the keys. They were on your dresser and the Harley logo is hard to miss. He also knew where you'd stored the bike."

"I've been thinking the same thing," Dottie said. "The gang members would recognize the car. They wouldn't expect to see him on a motorcycle."

Ernest was waiting for them at the house. It was hard not to miss him in his orange cargo shorts with bulging side pockets and matching vest. A magnifying glass stuck out the top pocket. His ears protruded from beneath a deerstalker hat.

"You look like you're ready for action," Dottie said.

Ernest beamed. "The lumber's been delivered and the work crew are finished for the day. So we have the place to ourselves." He unlocked the front door and the two women followed him into the house. "Come."

They climbed the narrow, winding stairs.

Ernest reached the attic first. "Well, well, well!"

When Dottie joined Ernest, her heart sank. The only items left were a few old pieces of furniture and a wooden chest.

"They've cleared out," Mabel said. "Lock, stock, and barrel."

Ernest rubbed his hands together. "Let's take a look around. You never know what we might find." He unzipped one of the side pockets of his shorts and pulled out a handful of rubber gloves. "These are biogel neo-tech synthetic gloves."

Dottie looked at Ernest. "What are you talking about?"

He cleared his throat. "Well, some people are allergic to latex. So, to be on the safe side, I always use latex-free rubber gloves."

"Why do we need them?" Mabel said. "We aren't doing anything illegal."

"We don't want to contaminate evidence."

Dottie agreed. Best to play it safe.

They pulled on the gloves. Dottie started with the bathroom. The only things left were the bar of soap, hand towel and a roll of toilet paper. The toothbrush and toothpaste Ernest mentioned had disappeared. As she turned to leave, Dottie spotted a chain lying at the side of the toilet bowl. She picked it up and found a St. Christopher's medallion attached to it.

Her heart leapt when she recognized the slight dent on the left. Images of Woodstock crowded into her head. She and Fred were sleeping in a makeshift tent. The constant rain made everything soggy, including their shoes. A small St. Christopher medallion, caked in mud, was fastened to one of Fred's shoelaces. When they had reconnected last year, he still had his medallion but wore it on a chain around his neck.

Dottie walked over to Mabel. "I've found Fred's medallion." She showed it to Mabel.

"Are you sure it's his?"

Dottie nodded. Had Fred left it on purpose? Her eyes came to rest on the wooden chest. That would be a good place to leave a clue. She reached over and lifted the lid. The chest appeared empty. She ran her fingers over the bottom. Nothing.

"Wait!"

Dottie spun around to find Ernest rushing over to her. "Don't shout like that," she scolded.

"Your nerves are bad, Dottie. Are you taking those passion flower pills I sent you?"

Dottie gritted her teeth. "What is it, Ernest?"

"I have a flashlight." He thrust it into her hand. As Ernest nattered on about the superior quality of the flashlight, Dottie tuned him out and concentrated on the chest. All she could see were dead bugs on the bottom. She directed the beam along the sides of the chest and discovered a pencil lying on an iron seam that jutted out about half an inch. A piece of paper secured by an elastic band was wound around it.

Dottie unwrapped the paper. Her heart leapt when she recognized the familiar handwriting. "The note says *Being moved to Pauline's.* Any idea what it means, Ernest?"

His eyes lit up. "My favorite Italian restaurant. Great spaghetti and tofu balls.... Closed for renovations at the moment and won't be open for another week at least."

"Where is it?"

"Off Pope Avenue."

"Are we talking Savannah or Hilton Head?"

"Oh, sorry," Ernest said. "Keep forgetting you don't know the area. Hilton Head."

Dottie's heart raced. "Fred left that note. That's where he's been taken."

"What makes you so sure he wrote it?"

"The handwriting."

"A lot of people have similar handwriting."

Dottie glared at Ernest. "Fred wrote that note. It looks like he was brought here from the plantation house.

He must have heard them talking about moving him to Pauline's."

Ernest patted his lips with a forefinger. "And it would be a good place to hide someone. It's surrounded by trees and bushes."

Dottie picked up her phone. "I'm calling Sergeant Cooper."

She tapped her foot as the number rang out. When it switched to his answering service, Dottie's heart sank. She left a brief message. "This is Dottie Flowers. I've reason to believe Fred Fortune is being held at Pauline's restaurant off Pope Avenue on Hilton Head. Please call me right back."

She chewed her lip.

"Maybe you should speak to another officer," Mabel said.

"I'd rather not. Sergeant Cooper knows the details of the case."

Minutes felt like hours. Maybe they should check out the restaurant themselves. Dottie didn't relish facing the sergeant's wrath after the dressing down they got from him for taking it upon themselves to try to save Mabel and Harriet. But Fred's life could be in real danger.

As soon as she suggested it, Ernest's eyes shot open. "Are you crazy? If a gangster sees us, we'll be murdered on the spot!"

"I think we should go," Mabel said.

Dottie looked at Ernest. "Are you coming with us?"

Ernest's eyes darted back and forth. "I... I... don't... I... I can't...."

Beethoven's Fifth cut into his dithering. Dottie grabbed her phone.

"Got your message," Sergeant Cooper's voice rang in Dottie's ears. "What's happened."

Dottie gave him the details.

"We're on it. Stay put and leave your cell on," he instructed. He ended the call.

"You're off the hook, Ernest. The police are on their way to the restaurant. "

He took out a large white handkerchief from his pants pocket and mopped his brow. "I can't tell you how relieved I am, Dottie."

Dottie said, "Let's pray Fred's still alive."

Chapter Thirty-Three

Dottie paced back and forth across the attic. A cloud of smoke trailed behind her as she puffed on a cigarillo.

Ernest coughed and waved the smoke away. "No point hanging around here. The police have your cell number. There's a coffee shop around the corner."

"He's right," Mabel said. "Let's go."

Dottie sighed and followed them down the stairs. They threaded their way along the busy sidewalk until they reached Cafe Latte.

As they walked into the cafe, Dottie breathed in the welcome aroma of fresh-ground coffee beans. Dishes clattered in the kitchen; the hum of voices filled the air. Customers, mostly women, sipped on tall glasses of iced lattes, bulging shopping bags at their feet.

"My treat," Ernest said. "I know Dottie likes her coffee black. How about you, Mabel?"

"Triple cream and three sugars please."

Ernest looked aghast. "All that sugar is bad for you."

"I need the extra energy," Mabel explained.

"And think of the fat content in cream!"

Mabel studied the menu. Ernest shook his head and got in line.

The two women found an empty booth and sat down. "I wonder how long it'll take the police to check the restaurant," Dottie said.

"I expect they're already there. And once Fred's rescued, they'll hammer him with questions. It could take hours."

"Assuming they find him." Dottie wished she had Mabel's optimism.

A few minutes later, Ernest delivered their coffee, a cheese and cherry Danish and two muffins. He sat down and handed Mabel the Danish.

"You've just lectured me on my bad eating habits and now you buy me this." She took a large bite.

"Truth be told, I felt a bit guilty getting on your case," Ernest said. "A naughty treat doesn't do any harm, once in a while."

Dottie's stomach churned at the sight of the creamy filling and heavy glaze. "I'm glad it's not for me."

"I got you a wheat germ muffin."

Dottie wasn't hungry but picked away at it.

Savoring the dark roast coffee, Dottie was glad Ernest had suggested they come here. Far better than waiting around in a dusty old attic. She'd almost finished the coffee when her phone rang. Her eyes darted from Ernest to Mabel before she picked it up.

"Sergeant Cooper, Ma'am. Good news. We found Mr. Fortune inside the restaurant, unharmed."

A wave of relief swept over Dottie. "Thank God! Was Rick with him?"

"No, Ma'am." The sergeant cleared his throat. "We need to question Mr. Fortune. We'll call you to pick him up, but it'll be a while."

"I understand."

After the call ended, Dottie turned to her friends. Her voice cracked as she spoke. "Fred's free."

Mabel smiled. "That's wonderful news! At last I'll get to meet him. What about Rick?"

"He wasn't there."

Dottie sat back. "I can't believe it's over." She noticed Ernest's glum face as he stared into his coffee mug. "What's wrong?"

He glanced at her then looked away. "A lot on my mind. Must go. Got a meeting with some clients." He stood up.

"Thank you for everything you've done, Ernest," Dottie said.

He blushed. "What are friends for?" He tugged on his earlobe. "Do you think we could have dinner together? When things... er...quieten down?"

"See that!" Mabel cried as she pointed through the cafe window. Dottie and Ernest swung around.

Dottie furrowed her brow. "What are we supposed to be looking at, Mabel?"

"I swear I saw a dog in a bike helmet and goggles." Mabel shrugged. "I think I need to get my eyes checked."

Ernest looked at his watch. "I'm off. I'll be in touch."

After he left, Dottie turned to Mabel. "What was that all about?"

"I was trying to save you the embarrassment of having to say no to the dinner invitation."

Dottie shrugged. "He just doesn't get that I'm not interested. Anyway, enough of Ernest. We need to call at the grocery store and get some deli meat and bread for sandwiches. Then we'll go to Virginia's. "

"I'll call her." Mabel took out her cell.

Dottie suppressed a smile. "I'm impressed you remembered to charge your phone."

"After what we went through, I don't think I'll ever forget again."

Mabel spoke briefly with Virginia and hung up. "She suggested we pick up iced tea to go with the sandwiches. And we still have pizza. Fred'll be famished by the time we pick him up from the police station."

"Forget iced tea," Dottie said. "He'll want a cold beer."

Back in Hilton Head, they bought cold cuts, pickles, mayo, mustard, pumpernickel bread and beer. At Virginia's, they put the beer in the fridge and made sandwiches. Dottie wrote a *welcome-back,-Fred* note, added all their names and stuck it on the front door. Then she joined Mabel and Virginia in the living room.

"Scarlett's out shoppin'. She should be back in an hour or so," Virginia said. "Anyone fancy a game of cards?"

Mabel and Dottie shook their heads.

"They're showin' reruns of *Golden Girls,* Virginia said. "I'll go and watch them in my room."

"I want to finish my Danielle Steel novel," Mabel said. "What about you, Dottie?"

"I'll stay put."

Dottie felt jittery and wound up, like she was going to jump out of her skin. After flipping through a stack of Virginia's old *Elle* magazines, she lit a cigarillo and sat back in a comfortable armchair. Once more, her mind went back to last year when Fred had turned up on her doorstep.

To get re-acquainted, they'd gone out for dinner several times. As time went on, they developed a close friendship but nothing more. Yet memories of Woodstock lingered. It wasn't like Dottie to be sentimental, so why did a romance that had happened so long ago hold such a powerful grip?

Sunlight streamed through the windows making the living room uncomfortably warm. Dottie's eyelids grew heavy. She butted out the cigarillo and settled back in the armchair for a nap.

***

"Fred's here!" Mabel shouted from her bedroom. "The police just dropped him off."

Dottie sat up, blinked several times and checked her watch. It was already eight o'clock. The doorbell rang twice. She took a quick look at herself in the mirror above the fireplace. Her skin looked pasty. Too bad she didn't have time to put on some make-up. Taking a deep breath, she hurried into the hallway and opened the door. Fred stood on the mat, the note in his hand. Dottie's eyes welled with tears.

He grabbed Dottie and gave her a bear hug. "Am I glad to see you!"

She could feel his ribs through his sweat shirt. He'd lost weight since she'd last seen him a year ago, before he went to Rio.

Stepping back, he took a good look at her. A smile played on his lips. "You're still the best-looking woman I ever met."

Heat swept into her cheeks. When was the last time she'd blushed?

She noticed his ponytail had gone. "You got your hair cut."

"Working as a lawyer, I figured I'd better look the part."

His grey hair curled around the nape of his neck and fell in a wave across his forehead. She fought back the urge to run her fingers through it.

Fred's blue eyes were fixed on her face.

"Sorry, I was.... Your hair suits you." She cleared her throat. "Come on in. We've made sandwiches and there's cold beer in the fridge."

"Sounds great. The police grilled me for hours. It's been a long day."

"We were supposed to come and pick you up but no-one called. What happened?"

"One of the officers had business in the plantation so he drove me here." Fred looked down at his clothing. "I need a shower. But first I have to talk to you about Rick."

He followed Dottie into the living room and they sat on the sofa. Dottie turned to him. "So what's going on?"

"Rick's in danger."

"What do you mean?"

Feet clumped down the stairs. Mabel appeared and joined them in the living room. She smiled at Fred. "I'm Mabel. It's good to meet you face to face."

Fred returned the smile. "Likewise."

They shook hands.

"Come and sit down," Dottie said. "Fred's got something important to tell us about Rick."

Mabel sat opposite them. "Has something happened to him?"

"Not yet." Fred blew out a weary sigh. "Rick's planning to steal drugs from the lab tonight."

"That's what I was afraid of!"

At the sound of Virginia's voice, they all turned around.

Virginia rushed over to Fred and took his hand. "It's good seein' you again, Fred!" She peered at him. "You're lookin' a bit pale, but that's to be expected with all you've gone through."

She retrieved a packet of cigarettes from a side table and offered one to him. After he declined, she shook one out and lit it. "How did you find out about Rick's plan?'

"He slipped a note under the bedroom door." Fred glanced at Mabel. "At the house where we were being held."

Mabel looked puzzled. "If the hoodlums had caught him, how could he leave you a note?"

Fred sighed. "Let's not go there right now." He rubbed his hands over his face. "It's clear from the note that Rick expected those assholes to free me as soon as they got their hands on the drugs. He's living in la la land. Assuming he goes ahead and steals the drugs tonight, it won't end there. My guess is they'll keep threatening him to get him to steal more."

"You should call Rick right away, let him know you're free," Dottie said. "Then he'll have no reason to steal the drugs."

Virginia handed her cell phone to Fred and he punched in the number. After a short pause, he said, "Rick, it's almost nine, Friday evening. You're off the hook, buddy. The police found me. I'm at Virginia's house. Call her number when you get this." He turned to Virginia. "I need to borrow your car."

Virginia's eyebrows rose. "No problem, but why?"

"I have to go to the lab. If Rick's planning to steal the drugs tonight, my guess is he's working the evening shift, which ends at 11."

Dottie checked her watch. "That's more than two hours away. Why so early?"

"If Rick happens to come out earlier, or changes his mind, I want to be there."

"I'm coming with you."

"No way!"

Dottie tried to sound more confident than she felt. "Is the lab hidden from the road?"

Fred grasped her arm and looked into her eyes. "You're not getting involved. It's too dangerous."

"You don't have a choice."

A puzzled look crossed Fred's face. "What are you talking about?"

"Virginia's car's a stick shift. Unless you learned in Rio, you've never driven standard."

"It can't be that difficult."

"A big problem if you need to make a fast getaway."

Fred sighed. "Okay, you win."

"Is there anywhere we can hide the car?"

"When I dropped off Rick one time, I noticed the area outside the security section of the lab has plenty of trees and bushes."

"Let's go before it gets dark." Dottie stood up.

"I'll stay with Scarlett," Virginia said. "What about you, Mabel?"

"I'm not missing this. I'll bring those sandwiches we made for you, Fred, and some canned drinks. And I'll take my e-reader. Time will just sail by."

Fred shook his head but said nothing.

***

Finding a hiding place for the car turned out to be easy. Dottie turned into a small clearing with a view of the employee parking lot and the lab. She switched off the engine, rolled down the window and looked over the vehicles in the car park. There was no sign of the Harley. Was it possible Rick had changed his mind?

Nobody spoke. Through the open car window, Dottie breathed in the pungent smell of damp earth. As darkness fell, the clawed branches of the ancient live oaks reminded Dottie of monsters in a childhood fairy tale.

Half an hour later, Mabel handed out sandwiches and drinks. As they ate, Mabel said, "Fred, there's something I'm curious about. At one point, Harriet and I were locked in some broken-down old house in a crummy room. I found a fountain pen with a Brazilian brand name on it..."

"It's mine. I wondered what happened to it," Fred said.

"So you were there!"

"Sure was. What a dump! A man called Lucas provided food—if the garbage he gave me could be called that."

"He was murdered by the River Ghosts."

"I'm not surprised," Fred said. "I overheard him and Rasta arguing. I only caught part of it but I heard Rasta accuse Lucas of double dealing."

After they'd eaten, Dottie read for a while, using her portable reading light, then fell into a light doze. The distant thunder wakened her. She shuddered when a series of booms heralded a storm, and rolled up the window.

Within minutes, wind gusted through the trees and sheets of rain pounded the car roof. She checked her watch. It was just after eleven o'clock.

As Dottie watched the storm, lightning flashed over something metallic. A second flash revealed the shiny fender of a motorcycle. Her pulse began to race. "Rick's here."

"How do you know?" Fred demanded.

"I just saw the Harley." Dottie pointed to the employee parking lot entrance. "It's not in the parking lot, it's on this side of the gate, quite close to our car."

Another thunderclap sounded overhead followed by a series of popping sounds.

"That sounds like fireworks," Dottie said.

"Get down!" Fred yelled. "That's not fireworks. It's gunfire!"

Chapter Thirty-Four

Dottie crouched and wrapped her arms around her head. The passenger door clicked open. When she saw Fred getting out of the car, her throat constricted. "Where are you going?"

He slammed the door and took off without a word.

Dottie steeled herself, expecting to hear more shots. "Can you see anything out your window, Mabel?'

"Just foliage. I'll keep looking."

It stopped raining as abruptly as it began. Dottie lowered the window again. A few minutes later, she heard the rustle of leaves. She glanced out the window and saw Fred stagger to the car, half carrying a man who leaned on his shoulder.

Dottie stuck her head out. "What happened?"

"Rick's been shot," Fred said. "He needs to lie down."

Dottie jumped from the car and opened the hatchback. The trunk was littered with an assortment of gardening magazines, and an old pillow. She pushed the magazines to one side while Mabel opened one of the rear doors and folded down the seat. With great care, they lifted Rick into the car and placed the pillow under his head. His face contorted with pain as they removed his blood-soaked jacket.

"Let me take a look." Mabel ripped open Rick's sweater. "He's been shot in the shoulder. Give me your shirt, Dottie." Thankful she wore a tank top underneath, Dottie took off her shirt and handed it to Mabel. Rick groaned in agony when Mabel pressed the shirt over his wound to stop the bleeding.

Dottie looked at Fred. "Where was he?"

"Lying on the ground. There's a trail of blood from the bike."

Rick groaned again. Dottie's thoughts raced through her head. They had to get him to a hospital but if those slimeballs saw a car appear from the woods, they'd assume Rick was in it. *Maybe I could act as a decoy.*

She noticed Fred's windbreaker lying on the passenger seat. It was navy blue, like Rick's. She pulled on the jacket, zipped it up and flicked the hood over her head. The bike keys jangled as she removed them from Rick's jacket.

Fred turned around. "What are you... oh, no you don't."

"Rick's lost a lot of blood. We need to move fast," Dottie said. "I'm going to drive the bike onto the main road. If those goons see the Harley they'll assume I'm Rick and follow me. Mabel, do you know where the hospital is?"

"Yes. I had to drive Virginia to emergency two years ago."

Dottie got out of the car. She turned to Fred. "Keep pressure on Rick's wound."

"You'll get killed," Fred protested. "This is crazy..."

Before Fred had a chance to stop her, Dottie ran toward the bike. When she reached the edge of the wooded area, she hid behind a bush and glanced around. Light from the employee parking lot spilled onto the clearing.

At first, she didn't notice anything unusual. Then she spotted the hood of a car jutting out from some bushes about twenty yards away. She guessed it was the goons' car. Dottie ran across the clearing, climbed on the bike and started up the engine. Within seconds, two men headed toward her, guns pointed. She accelerated and the bike leapt forward. Shots rang out. As she exited onto the main road, a bullet ricocheted off the back fender of the Harley.

When she reached the traffic lights, Dottie took deep breaths to slow her pounding heart. As soon as the light changed to green, she turned left. She needed to drive around for at least half an hour to give the others time to reach the hospital.

She drove for about ten minutes with no sign of the SUV. Maybe they're headed in the opposite direction, she reasoned. Anyway, on a busy road like this she should be safe. Or was she? Her mouth went dry. If Rick had stolen the drugs, where would he have stashed them? The saddle bags!

Dottie pulled over to the side of the road and checked. One of the bags was empty; the other held two bulging Ziploc bags. Fearing the mobsters might appear at any moment, she jumped back on the bike and pulled back onto the road.

Somehow she had to get rid of the drugs. But how?

Within a few minutes, the scenery changed to wide grassy spaces and parkland. Traffic eased but the road was poorly lit. She glanced to her left and right but couldn't see any houses or side streets. Her spirits rose when she realized hers was the only vehicle on the road. Was it possible she'd lost them?

Her optimism was short lived. An SUV appeared around a sharp bend, sped up and stayed on her tail. Within minutes, it pulled out, accelerated and moved alongside the Harley. From the corner of her eye, Dottie saw a handgun pointed at her through the open car window. Shots exploded.

As she swerved to avoid the gunfire, the wheels slipped in the gravel at the roadside. Dottie fought to keep the bike under control. Narrowly avoiding a ditch, she steered onto a flat grassy area, squeezed the brake lever and jerked to a stop.

The SUV bumped over the grass and stopped a few yards in front of Dottie. Two men jumped out and rushed toward her.

Her legs trembled as she climbed off the bike and threw back the hood of her jacket, shaking her long hair free. "What's going on?" she said, struggling to keep the fear out of her voice. The men stopped in their tracks.

After a short pause, the younger man sneered and pulled his gun. "The game's over, lady." The bike lights caught the flash of a diamond in his nose.

The second man, olive-skinned with hair in dreadlocks, scowled at his partner. "Get the drugs out of the saddlebags, Stud. Let's get out of here." This must be Rasta, Dottie realized.

At that moment, a siren wailed. A patrol car pulled over to the side of the road, lights flashing. Thank God the police are here! Two officers climbed out of the cruiser. Rasta and Stud shot at the police, turned and ran toward a thicket. The officers gave chase, and the men disappeared down a hill, in a hail of gunfire.

Dottie's relief was quickly replaced with panic. If they searched the bike, they'd find the prescription drugs inside the saddlebag. How would she explain that to the police?

Before she had a chance to figure something out, brakes screeched and a horn blared. A livestock trailer turned the corner at breakneck speed. It wobbled then veered off the road and headed straight toward them. Dottie ran for cover. She watched in shock as the trailer bounced over the grass, caught the bike's tailpipe and sent it spinning on its side before it smashed into the SUV. Finally the truck crashed into a large tree. It toppled onto its side with a thud and the back door flew open. A cacophony of squeals erupted as pigs leapt out of the truck and bolted in all directions.

Chapter Thirty-Five

Within minutes, four more squad cars, an ambulance and a fire truck pulled up, sirens wailing and lights flashing. Police officers, fire personnel and paramedics rushed over to the truck. Taking advantage of the confusion, Dottie dashed over to the bike, stuffed the Ziploc bags into the windbreaker pockets, and ran over to the damaged SUV. The passenger window was rolled down.

Dottie's heart battered against her chest as she removed the first bag from the pocket and unzipped it. She reached through the open window, and shook the bag. She heard the soft thud as the containers of drugs fell to the floor. She repeated the procedure with the second bag. When she got back to the bike, she tried to light a cigarillo. Her hands shook so hard it took three attempts.

Two officers headed over to Dottie. By now, the air was permeated with a combination of exhaust fumes, gunpowder, and the stink of pigs. The younger officer, his red hair in stark contrast to his pale freckled skin, stepped in front of her. "Ma'am what happened here? Are you all right?"

Gripping the cigarillo, Dottie flung out her hand. "Officer, I was out for an evening ride on my Harley, when those two jerks shot at me and ran me off the road." Dottie pointed to Rasta and Stud, who were now being escorted toward a squad car, in handcuffs.

The policeman cleared his throat. "Have you seen either of the men before?"

"No."

"Do you have any idea why they would try to run you off the road and pull guns on you?"

Dottie fluttered her eyelashes as though blinking back tears. "No idea at all."

The second officer broke in after checking the bike. "You've got a big dent in one of the fenders and a coupla bullet holes. But it should be all right to drive. If you have no objection, Ma'am, we'd like to take a look inside your saddle bags."

Why did they want to search the bike? Had Rasta and Stud told the officers that one of the bike's saddle bags contained stolen drugs?

The two men righted the bike then searched the bags. Dottie crossed her fingers. What if she'd left a package behind?

She breathed a sigh of relief when a few moments later, one of them said, "Nothing here. Let's check the SUV. By the way, did anyone call for help in rounding up the hogs?"

"Yeah. The animal rescue people have been contacted. Should get here any time now."

The officers headed to the smashed SUV. Dottie smiled to herself and took a long draw on the cigarillo. One of the cops opened the driver's door and looked inside the car. He stood up, turned, and spoke rapidly to his colleague. They pulled on plastic gloves and started to remove the drugs from the SUV.

Dottie glanced over to the truck. The driver had been rescued. He lay on a stretcher, which the medics were loading into the ambulance. A few minutes later, the ambulance pulled onto the road and drove away.

The red-headed policeman walked over to her. "Ma'am, you'll have to come down to the sheriff's office."

She squished her cigarillo under her shoe. "What on earth for? What's going on?"

"You need to make a statement."

"I have to make a phone call first."

"Go ahead but keep it short."

Dottie walked out of earshot and phoned Mabel. "What's happening with Rick?"

"Dottie, thank goodness you've called! Rick's in surgery. It doesn't look good. He lost a lot of blood. Virginia's frantic." Mabel paused. "Fred's stepped outside for a cigarette. He's really worried about you."

"I'm fine but can't talk right now."

"What should I tell Fred?"

"Stud and Rasta have been arrested. I have to go to the sheriff's office to make a statement, so I can't stay on the line." The grunts and squeals grew louder. Dottie turned to see pigs stampeding toward her.

"What are those dreadful noises? If I didn't know better, I'd swear you were on a farm."

"It's pigs!" Dottie yelled as a pig almost ran over her foot.

"Pigs?"

The policeman walked over to her and cleared his throat. "Let's go, Ma'am. First, we need to make sure the bike is operational. Then you'll follow the squad car."

"I'll call you later, Mabel."

"But wait—"

Dottie turned off the phone. She climbed onto the bike and fired up the engine.

The officer nodded and walked off.

As she pulled up behind the squad car, she checked her mirror. Another one was right behind her.

Rasta and Stud had been arrested and she'd managed to dump the drugs in their SUV, but one major problem remained. She'd reported to the Harley rental company that the bike had been stolen. Now here she was driving it. How on earth would she explain that to the police?

Chapter Thirty-Six

When Dottie walked into the hospital almost two hours later, it was past one. Mabel, Fred and Scarlett were the only people in the waiting room.

"Am I glad you're here!" Mabel said.

Fred stood up and hugged Dottie. His face was drawn.

"So, how's Rick?" she said.

"Still haven't heard." He ran his hands through his hair. "He's in bad shape and may not pull through."

"I'm so sorry, Fred."

Fred's voice shook. "Rick's always lived on the edge. Looks like he went too far this time."

With a sigh, he sat down again. "Dottie, tell me what's going on. Why were the police questioning you? And what's this about hogs?"

Dottie sat down between Fred and Mabel and told them everything.

"Let me see if I got this straight," Scarlett said. "First, you're chased by gangsters who run you off the road and threaten you with guns. A truck overturns and you're surrounded by pigs. And then you plant the drugs in the creeps' SUV."

"It sounds farfetched, I know."

Fred narrowed his eyes. "Did the police believe your story?"

"I have a feeling they'll want me back for more questioning. I'll explain later, but right now, tell me what happened after I left."

"While we were en route, I phoned the hospital and told them to expect Rick," Fred said. "By the time we got to emergency, a team of nurses and doctors was waiting."

Heels tapped along the hallway that led to the waiting room. Virginia walked in, looking pale with dark shadows under her eyes.

"What did the doctors say?" Fred said.

"The surgery went well, but the surgeon said the first twenty four hours are critical."

Fred nodded. "We could be here all night." He stood up. "Can I get you something, Virginia? You look wiped."

"Maybe something cold, liked iced tea."

"Right. I'm going to grab a coffee. Anyone else want one?"

"I'd love a black coffee." Dottie said.

Mabel said, "A can of coke or ginger ale, please....Do you think you could get me a chocolate bar as well?"

Scarlett stood up. "I'll give you a hand, Fred."

After they'd left, Virginia dropped into the chair vacated by Fred.

"This has been a very rough day for you," Mabel said.

"It's made me realize how important Rick is to me." A muffled sob escaped Virginia's lips. "I don't know how I'll cope if he doesn't make it."

Mabel put her arm around Virginia. "I'm pulling for him."

Dottie patted Virginia's arm. "We all are."

Virginia dabbed her eyes with a tissue. "Thanks."

Dottie turned to a pile of magazines that lay on the table next to her. Maybe a good article would keep her mind occupied. She put on her rhinestone glasses and flipped through the well-thumbed magazines. Nothing caught her attention. Yawning, she took off her glasses. If I stay in this overheated room much longer, I'll fall asleep. Her eyes began to close.

***

"Sorry we took so long." At the sound of Fred's voice, Dottie jerked awake. "We had trouble finding a vending machine that worked."

Fred handed iced tea to Virginia. "Any news?"

"Nothing."

They sipped their drinks in silence. A while later, a young nurse in flowered scrubs with a stethoscope around her neck popped her head around the waiting room door. "Mrs. Makefield?"

"That's me."

"Mr. Fortune's awake. He's asking for you."

Virginia returned a short time later, a stunned expression on her face.

Fred looked at her. "How's the patient?"

Virginia shook her head, as if to clear it. "He's still groggy. He's hooked up to IV bags, and other paraphernalia."

"Are you all right, Virginia?" Mabel said. "You look as though you're in shock."

Virginia sat down. "Do I? Fact is..." She leaned forward, a smile hovering on her lips. "Rick's asked me to marry him once this business is cleared up."

Scarlett gripped the armrests of her chair. "He's after your money, Ginny."

"Are you sure he knew it was you?" Mabel said. "Sometimes people are confused when they're coming out of the anesthetic. I remember my Uncle Enoch had an operation for a hernia, and when he was still half asleep he kept calling his wife Arabella. Auntie Dylis found out later that Arabella and Uncle Enoch were lovers."

Before Mabel had the chance to continue her story, the nurse reappeared. "Mrs. Makefield, can you please come with me."

Virginia leapt out of the chair and rushed over to the nurse. "Has something happened?"

She placed her hand on Virginia's arm. "Didn't mean to alarm you. Mr. Fortune has something to tell you." The two women left.

No one spoke for a few minutes.

"Do you think Virginia will accept the marriage proposal?" Mabel said.

"Don't even go there!" Scarlett looked at Fred. "Ginny's very susceptible to Rick's charm."

He waved his hand. "No need to explain. I know what he's like."

They settled back for another wait. Dottie checked her watch. It was already after two.

By the time Virginia returned, Fred and Scarlett had nodded off. Mabel was snoring, her mouth sagged open.

Dottie had managed to stay awake. "Is Rick okay, Virginia?"

"So so. I've got things to tell y'all."

Dottie shook Mabel's arm gently. Mabel opened her eyes, yawned, and sat up in the chair.

Dottie nudged Fred. He blinked and looked around. "What's happening?"

"Virginia wants to talk to us."

Virginia pulled up a chair opposite them and sat down. "Our suspicions about Rick were right. "He's admitted he's involved with the River Ghosts."

Fred sighed. "I was afraid of that."

"Rick agreed to steal the prescription drugs in exchange for Fred's release."

Scarlett said, "And he believed they'd keep their word? What an idiot."

Virginia glared at her sister. "I haven't finished. After he'd agreed to do this, Rick overheard them talkin'. Seems Rasta wanted Rick to continue stealin' drugs from the lab. Rick confronted Rasta. Told him he'd go through with this robbery to pay his debt, but that's all."

Dottie was curious. "What was Rasta's reaction?"

"Insisted they'd let Fred go once they had the drugs. But if Rick backed out, his brother would be killed. Rick panicked."

"What happened after the robbery?" Dottie said.

"Rasta and Stud were waiting in their car," Virginia said. "The employee parkin' lot is very busy at the end of a shift, so Rick parked outside the gate where he'd be less conspicuous. When he came out, he put the drugs into the bike's saddlebag. The plan was that when all the employees had left, the crooks would collect their booty and leave."

"What went wrong?"

"By the time Rick came out of the lab and transferred the drugs to the saddlebag, the stupidity of what he'd done hit home. There was no way these crooks were going to release Fred. He was their bargaining chip."

"Pity it didn't occur to him before he stole the drugs," Scarlett's voice dripped with sarcasm.

Virginia glared at her sister. "He decided to go straight to the police and confess everything. When he got on the bike, Rasta and Stud ran toward him, guns drawn. They began to fire. He ducked. The shot caught him in the shoulder but he managed to get off the bike and stagger part way into the woods."

"So why didn't they grab the drugs and leave?"

"Rick thinks they saw someone drive out of the parking lot. There are always a few stragglers at the end of a shift. It would have been too risky to remove them from the saddlebag until they were sure the parking lot was empty."

Everyone fell silent. Finally, Virginia said, "Let's go back to my house. There's no point stayin' here. Rick's being well taken care of."

"I'll drive," Scarlett said, then turned to Dottie. "I guess you'll park the bike at Mary-Lou's place and walk over."

Fred grinned at Dottie. "Mind if I hitch a ride with you?"

"Why not?"

"I'm hungry," Mabel said. "I think there's still leftover pizza in the fridge."

"And I've got a pot of chicken soup I took out of the freezer earlier," Virginia added.

Fred and Dottie hung back as the others walked toward the elevator. "If Rick confesses, he'll tell the police he stole the bike," Fred said.

"I know....I'd reported the theft to the rental company who of course told the police."

"So you were riding a bike you claim had been stolen. How did you explain that?"

"I told the police I'd found the bike."

"What?"

"I said I'd parked it in Mary Lou's neighbor's yard by mistake. In the dark the houses looked identical."

"How did they respond?"

"They didn't say much. They wanted to know if I'd told the rental company I'd found the bike. I said I planned to phone them as soon as I was allowed to leave."

"What did the rental company say when you told them?"

"They were happy to know the bike's safe. I told them how sorry I was for making such a dumb mistake."

Fred laughed. "Sounds like you covered your tracks."

"I guess I've still got what it takes."

"And then some." Fred took Dottie by the arm and looked into her eyes. You're all I ever wanted. You know that, don't you."

Dottie felt a rush of heat to her face.

"Hey, you two. Hurry up. I'm holding the elevator!" Mabel called out.

"Let's go," Dottie said.

After eating, they relaxed by the living room fire and polished off a few bottles of wine. At four a.m., Virginia insisted everyone stay for what remained of the night. "There's plenty of room. Dottie, you can sleep in Mabel's room. It's got twin beds. And Fred, you take the back bedroom."

They all trudged off to bed.

The following morning, Scarlett got up around ten thirty, prepared coffee and glanced through the local paper. The others trailed in, helped themselves to coffee and sat at the kitchen table.

Mabel looked at Virginia. "Did you call the hospital?"

"Yes. Rick had a restless night. He's sleeping right now."

Scarlett sipped her coffee. "What's on your agenda today, Ginny?"

"The hospital. Rick and I need to have a long talk, if he's up to it."

"You're not going to marry him, I hope!"

"You'll have to wait and see," Virginia snapped.

"No need to get into a snit. How about you, Fred? I suppose you're thinking about returning to Rio."

"Sure am. After I know Rick's going to be okay."

Dottie's coffee tasted bitter all of a sudden.

Virginia picked up her mug. "How long are you plannin' to stay in Rio, Fred?"

"I have another eight months to go on my contract." Fred looked at Dottie. "I'd like to work in the Toronto area when I return to Canada."

Dottie smiled to herself.

Virginia looked at Dottie. "I guess you and Mabel will be headin' home soon."

Dottie nodded. "Fall's a busy season in real estate."

"My tai chi classes start next week," Mabel said.

That was news to Dottie. "I didn't know you'd signed up for tai chi."

"My neighbor, Florida, swears by it. She's become a vegetarian, like her instructor."

Scarlett said, "Are you thinking of giving up meat, Mabel?"

"I might."

Dottie smiled. Mabel, a vegetarian?

"What happened to the Paeleo diet?"

"I need to do more research on it."

Dottie's cell phone rang. When caller ID showed Ernest's name, she let it go. She couldn't put him off much longer, but now wasn't the time.

Chapter Thirty-Seven

Later that morning, Dottie and Mabel rode back to Savannah to return the rental bike. As soon as they got back to the Hampton Inn, Dottie booked two flights to Toronto for the next afternoon.

"So much has happened in two weeks. I feel as though I've been here for ages," Mabel said.

"Unfortunately we'll have to come back when those creeps go on trial."

"That could be months from now…" Why don't we go out for one last lunch?" Mabel's eyes sparkled. "I've always wanted to try the Olde Pink House. I fancy another taste of southern hospitality before we head home."

"Excellent idea. I'll book a table."

Dottie found the phone number in the directory and was about to key it in when her iPhone rang. It was Virginia.

"Dottie, glad I caught you."

"You sound stressed. Is Rick okay?"

"He's makin' good progress. Fred came in to see him while I was there… Rick and I had a long chat today. He's gung ho on confessin' everythin' to the police. I've been on the phone to his lawyer. He's goin' to the hospital to meet with Rick."

Dottie bit her lip. How would the police react when they discovered she'd lied to them?

Virginia said, "This will make things awkward for you, Dottie. I know you tried to help Rick by stretchin' the truth a little."

"When are the police going to question him?"

"This afternoon."

"Call me when they're finished."

Dottie ended the call and turned to Mabel. "Rick's planning to confess."

"Which means they'll want to question you again. You were just looking out for Rick. Surely that will go in your favor."

"I doubt it. Let's face it, Mabel, I'm in big trouble."

***

The phone rang an hour later and Dottie answered right away. "What happened, Virginia?"

"It's Ernest."

Dottie sighed. "Sorry, Ernest. I was expecting another call."

"Did you get my message?"

"Things have been rather hectic."

"Oh." He sounded deflated. "I wanted to take you out for dinner tonight. It's very important I see you."

"Dinner? Tonight? The thing is, Ernest—"

Mabel grabbed Dottie's phone. "Dottie will call you right back, Ernest."

"What are you doing?"

"Ernest's brother's a criminal lawyer in Savannah, right?"

"Yes. But I don't see—"

"You need legal advice, Dottie. Accept Ernest's invitation and find out if his brother will represent you."

"That seems so calculating and cold blooded."

"Once you tell Ernest everything, I'm sure he'll want to help."

Dottie lit a cigarillo and inhaled deeply. "It's worth a try, I suppose."

Her phone rang again. It was Virginia.

"The police grilled Rick for over an hour. Thank God he has a good lawyer! They would have stayed longer if the nurse hadn't kicked them out."

Dottie took a long draw on the cigarillo. "So now they'll want to question me."

"Sorry about this, Dottie."

"I can handle it. I've been questioned twice by the police since I got to Savannah. I'm getting used to it."

As soon as she got off the phone, she called Ernest. "Sorry. I had to take another call. Now, about dinner tonight...."

Chapter Thirty-Eight

Dottie slipped on her black silk pants and white crocheted top with a hint of cleavage, along with a pair of strappy high-heeled sandals. She took a critical look at herself in the long mirror behind the closet door. The outfit needed a splash of color. Red lipstick would do the trick. When Ernest picked her up from the Hampton Inn wearing jeans and a red and green checked shirt, Dottie realized she was way overdressed.

"I'm going to take you to one of my favorite restaurants," he said. A few minutes later, he pulled up in front of *Vegan Heaven.*

After they were seated, Ernest rubbed his hands together. "Now, what would you like to drink?" He put on a pair of reading glasses and peered at the drinks menu. "They have sweetened or unsweetened iced tea, of course. Or would you prefer an alcoholic beverage?"

Was Ernest a teetotaler? Maybe she should play it safe and order iced tea. On the other hand, a drink might bolster her courage. "A glass of red wine would be perfect."

"I'll have the same. Truth is, I've never been an imbiber. Apart from the odd brandy and dry ginger I'd have with mother." Ernest smiled. "But this is a special occasion. Why don't you order the wine, Dottie?'

She chose a full-bodied Shiraz.

When the waiter asked "A six ounce or nine ounce glass?" Ernest interjected to say a six ounce glass would be more than sufficient. Dottie glanced away to hide her disappointment.

Once the wine was served, they settled back to enjoy it and opened their menus. Although Dottie was vegetarian by preference, she enjoyed fish on occasion. Her eyes scanned the menu: tomato protein soup, avocado fries, world peace cookies, but no fish. After a thorough search, she selected corn tacos filled with salsa, guacamole and walnut refried beans along with a side salad of organic greens. Ernest chose a soy burger with jicama fries.

During dinner, Ernest prattled away as usual. In between raves about the burger, he told stories about construction jobs he'd undertaken in the distant past, near past and the ones he was currently working on.

Dottie stifled yawns behind her napkin and waited for the right moment to ask for his assistance. It came after the dessert was served.

As Dottie nibbled one of the Super Seed Chocolate Protein Bites that Ernest had recommended, he said, "So, Dottie, please tell me what is going on. We have not spoken since Fred was rescued."

She took a deep breath and told Ernest about Rick's predicament; that he'd been forced to steal narcotics in order to secure his brother, Fred's, release.

A horrified look spread across Ernest's face. "He stole drugs?"

"He confessed to the police a few hours ago from his hospital bed."

"I should hope so! Why is he in hospital?"

"He was shot by one of the goons."

"Humph! You know what they say. 'If you lie with dogs, you get fleas.' Seems to me Rick has brought this on himself by mixing with the wrong type."

"Don't you think you're being a bit hasty, Ernest? Wouldn't you do the same for your brother if he'd been kidnapped?"

Ernest put his wine glass down. "Rick should have contacted the authorities rather than take matters into his own hands."

"You may be right, but when mobsters are holding your brother at gunpoint, you would have second thoughts."

Ernest shook his head. "It goes right against the grain, Dottie."

This wasn't going well. When the waiter asked if they'd like another glass of wine, Dottie nodded and ordered a nine ounce. Ernest raised his eyebrows but settled on mineral water.

When the drinks arrived, Dottie took a large gulp of wine. "Ernest. I've got myself in a tight spot. I'm hoping you can help."

"I'll do my best. Please tell me what I can do."

Dottie swallowed several mouthfuls of wine and held on to the glass. She told Ernest that she, Mabel and Fred had gone to the lab to try to stop Rick.

"What happened?"

"Unfortunately, we were too late. We heard gunshots and Fred found his brother lying on the ground, badly wounded. Fred carried Rick back to our car."

Ernest leaned across the table. "Go on."

"I put on Fred's jacket, which looked like Rick's, pulled the hood over my head and ran to the bike. I figured the mobsters would follow me if they thought I was Rick. That would give Mabel time to get Rick to hospital. I managed to get away but eventually they caught up." Dottie explained the rest of the story.

Ernest's eyes grew wide with horror. "You aided and abetted a criminal."

"That's right."

Ernest looked at her over his half moon glasses. "And you lied to the police."

Dottie nodded.

He stuck his chin in the air and placed his elbows on the table, lacing his fingers together. "I don't see how I can help. The thing is, Dottie, tonight was going to be a special occasion. I was planning to ask you to marry me."

Oh, shit! She drained her glass.

"I lived with my dear mother until she died just over a year ago. She wanted me to find the right lady, get married and settle down. Those were her last words to me." He pulled out an oversized white handkerchief from his breast pocket and dabbed his eyes.

"I don't know what to say, Ernest."

He folded his handkerchief and put it away. He looked at her with a pained expression on his face. "Until this moment, I thought you were that lady."

Dottie held her breath. She covered her mouth with her hand and fought the urge to laugh.

After a lengthy silence, Ernest spoke. "Your confession came as a shock. Perhaps I overreacted. Though you're not the kind of woman I could marry, we are friends. You wanted my help, Dottie. What did you have in mind?"

"I appreciate your integrity, Ernest." She took a deep breath. "You told me your brother is a criminal lawyer. Do you think he'd represent me?"

Ernest didn't answer.

A voice broke the silence. "Your bill, sir."

Ernest glanced at the waiter. "Thank you."

After the waiter left, Ernest looked at Dottie. "Here is what I am going to do. Because I believe you are a good person who somehow got led astray, I am willing to talk to Oscar."

"Thank you." Dottie went limp with relief.

"I presume the police are going to question you again. When will this take place?"

"Tomorrow morning at eleven."

They drove back to the Hampton Inn in silence. As Dottie climbed out of the car, Ernest said, "I'll call Oscar when I get home and get back to you."

By the time Dottie got to the suite, she felt the early symptoms of a migraine and took pills right away.

"So what happened?" Mabel said.

"Ernest is going to speak with his brother tonight."

"From the tone of your voice, I gather things didn't go as planned."

"You got that right. But that's not all." Dottie told Mabel about the marriage proposal.

"Good grief! I know he's been chasing you, but I didn't see that coming." Mabel smiled. "I'll make us a cup of Earl Grey tea."

Within minutes, she handed Dottie a Styrofoam cup of hot water with a tea bag floating inside. "It's not the same as a teapot and loose leaf tea, but it'll do."

Dottie's cell rang. It was Ernest.

"You're in luck," Ernest said. "Oscar's prepared to represent you. But his fees are steep."

"Do you know what they are?"

"He wants a retainer of $5000 upfront. And he charges $800 an hour for his services."

Dottie took a deep breath. "Fine."

"He'll meet you at your hotel tomorrow morning at eight. There are a lot of details to discuss before the interrogation."

"Thank you."

"I must say, Oscar was more sympathetic than I expected, but then again, he is used to dealing with lawbreakers."

"You reacted like any upright citizen would." Dottie needed to end this conversation. "I'd better go. I need to get a good night's sleep. Thanks again, Ernest."

"I've been thinking a lot about my previous comments. I didn't show any understanding or compassion. It's a character flaw I need to work on... Maybe we could meet after your police interview. Have some lunch and talk."

"I'm sorry, Ernest. I can't. We're flying back to Toronto tomorrow afternoon."

"Oh." His voice sounded flat. "Will you at least let me know how the interview goes?"

"Of course."

"Good luck, Dottie." She heard the phone click.

Dottie decided to pay the retainer fee by credit card. Before she went to bed, she spoke with a Visa representative to let them know about her proposed $5000 transaction. Before she drifted off to sleep, she thought, why didn't I take my father's advice all those years ago and go into law?

Chapter Thirty-Nine

The next morning, Oscar Palmertree, clutching a scuffed brown briefcase, met Dottie in the hotel lobby. As they shook hands, Dottie couldn't believe how little he resembled his brother. He was at least six inches taller than Ernest, and portly. His untidy white hair stuck out in all directions like the proverbial mad scientist. He wore a red and black tartan jacket over a black silk waistcoat, and a red bow tie. Buttoned over his ample belly, the jacket looked as though it was about to burst open.

He peered at Dottie over a pair of round gold-rimmed glasses. "We've got a lot of work to do before your interview, Mrs. Flowers." He glanced around. "But not here. The lobby's too busy."

"We have a suite upstairs."

"Perfect! Let's go."

Once they were settled, Dottie said, "Before we begin, I'd like to pay the retainer with Visa, please."

Oscar rummaged in his briefcase and pulled out a mobile credit card reader. When the transaction was finished, Oscar placed the reader back in his briefcase, and handed a receipt to Dottie. "Thank you. Now, let's get started. We'll use our formal names at the interview but while we're working together, I prefer to use given names if that's all right with you."

"Of course."

"Good! Now I need you to tell me in your own words exactly what happened."

***

After two intense hours, Dottie felt more comfortable about the upcoming interview. They left the Hampton Inn at ten thirty and arrived at the police station a few minutes later.

Just before they entered, Oscar said, "Remember, Dottie, don't answer any questions until I give you the go ahead. The interview will be recorded."

A female police officer ushered them into a windowless interview room that smelled of stale cigarettes, then left. A coffee-stained table sat in the middle of the room. A well-worn office chair had been placed behind the table and in front were two grubby-looking white plastic chairs. Did all interview rooms smell and look the same? she wondered.

After they were seated, a tall thin man with hunched shoulders walked in, carrying a file folder and a large coffee cup. A frown creased his forehead.

As he glanced over, his eyes widened. "Well, well. Oscar Palmertree."

"Detective Wheaton. It's been a while."

"You're representing Mrs. Flowers." It sounded more like a statement than a question.

"Indeed I am."

The detective looked as though he were about to say something but changed his mind.

After introducing himself to Dottie, Detective Wheaton sat down in the padded office chair and glanced through the contents of the file folder.

He closed the folder and looked at Dottie. "I assume you know the interview will be recorded?"

"Yes."

Detective Wheaton switched on the machine that sat on a table directly behind him. After reeling off the names of all present, along with the date and time of the interview, he cleared his throat. "Mrs. Flowers, a few days ago you made a statement to the police concerning your whereabouts on Friday, August 3. We've called you back today because of a few discrepancies that need clearing up."

He tapped the folder on the desk, and then opened it and examined one of the papers. "Let me refresh your memory. In your statement, you said you allowed Rick Fortune to borrow the rented Harley-Davidson bike because he was interested in buying one. You weren't sure of the exact date. You stated the bike disappeared but reappeared a day later where you'd originally parked it. You then stated you went for a ride on the bike and were forced off the road by two men in an SUV."

Dottie wished a hole would appear in the floor and swallow her. "Yes, that's what I said."

Sarcasm oozed off Detective Wheaton's tongue as he spoke. "We both know that your story was fabricated, don't we, Mrs. Flowers?"

"My client is not obliged to answer that, Detective."

The detective smirked at Oscar. Turning to Dottie, he said, "Mrs. Flowers, do you wish to make any changes to your original statement?"

Dottie glanced at Oscar. He gave her a brief nod.

Dottie summarized what had actually happened, glad that Oscar had made her repeat it several times before the interview.

When she described her plan to drive the bike from the lab grounds so the goons would follow her, the detective interrupted. "Why were you so sure they'd follow you?"

"I wore a man's jacket with the hood pulled over my head so they'd think I was Rick."

The detective muttered something under his breath and swallowed a large mouthful of coffee. "You say you removed the drugs from the saddlebag and placed them into the pockets of your jacket. How did they get from your jacket into the SUV?"

"As I said in my first statement, a truck carrying a load of pigs swerved onto the side of the road, knocked over the bike and crashed into the SUV. I took advantage of the confusion and dashed over to the SUV. The front window was open, so I dropped them inside the car."

The detective shook his head in disbelief.

After a brief pause, Detective Wheaton straightened himself up and looked directly at Dottie.

There was a hard edge to his voice. "Mrs. Flowers, you admit to lying in your first statement. That's obstruction of justice. You took the law into your own hands by getting involved in a crime. That's also a serious offence."

Oscar spoke up. "Detective Wheaton, Mrs. Flowers didn't stop to think about the legalities of what she was about to do when she drove the bike away. She acted out of a desire to help a fellow human being whom she feared was in serious trouble."

"You know as well as I do, Oscar, she committed crimes and lied about them."

Oscar sat back in his chair. He looked at Detective Wheaton. "Turn off the recorder, Detective."

The detective started to say something, then stopped. He turned off the machine.

Oscar said, "You know, Detective, we all make mistakes."

Detective Wheaton stared at Oscar for a few moments, then looked away.

"Years ago I remember a certain young off-duty cop who came upon a traffic accident." Oscar paused. "There was blood everywhere. He panicked and instead of stopping to help, he drove away."

Detective Wheaton's face grew ashen.

Oscar lowered his voice. "The point I'm trying to make, Mitch, is we've all done things we've regretted and have had to live with. Mrs. Flowers lied to get Rick Fortune off the hook because she knew he'd stolen the drugs in an attempt to save his brother's life. She put the drugs into the SUV to incriminate the two men who had allegedly shot Rick Fortune and were the alleged ring leaders behind a big drug smuggling operation. Mrs. Flowers may be misguided, but she is not a criminal."

Detective Wheaton cradled his coffee cup. He then put it down on the table and read through the file contents, making notes.

Finally, he turned on the recorder again. "I've given this matter serious thought, Mrs. Flowers. I believe your actions, though foolish, were an attempt to help a friend in trouble."

He paused and glanced at Oscar. "I'm going to let you off with a warning, but if you ever break the law again in my precinct, you'll be prosecuted to the full extent of the law. Have I made myself perfectly clear?"

"Yes, Detective."

"You'll be expected to appear in court when this case goes to trial."

"I understand, Detective."

Detective Wheaton turned off the recorder, replaced the papers in the file folder, nodded to Oscar and left the room.

***

Dottie joined Mabel back at the hotel.

"So, how did it go?"

"He let me go with a warning."

"Thank goodness!"

"Oscar was amazing." Dottie sighed. "Still, I feel bad about what happened last night with Ernest."

"Why? He's a self-righteous prig. Your fall off the pedestal is a blessing in disguise."

"What do you mean?"

"Think about it. You didn't have to turn down his marriage proposal."

Dottie laughed. "I hadn't thought of it like that."

"By the way, while I was waiting for you, I picked up the local Hilton Head paper. I found a short article about that truck driver with the load of pigs. Turns out he was high on marijuana. No wonder he lost control of the truck. He suffered scrapes and a few broken ribs. He's been charged with driving under the influence."

"He was fortunate to get out of that alive."

"Bet he won't be eating bacon for a while." Mabel stood up. "Right now, I need to pack."

"Just as well. I've done mine. I'm meeting Fred for coffee. Then it'll be time to head to the airport."

When Dottie arrived at the cafe, Fred was waiting. He stood up from the table and kissed her on the cheek.

"How did it go?" He sounded anxious.

"I got off with a warning"

"You were lucky!"

"Oscar convinced the police I was 'misguided,'" Dottie said.

Fred grinned. "Let me go get the coffees and pastries. Then we can talk."

Dottie watched Fred wind his way through the busy cafe to the counter. His scuffed running shoes, crumpled jeans and faded sweatshirt fit right in with the college crew. Except he was a good forty years older.

He was back within five minutes carrying a tray. He sat down opposite her and stirred sugar into his coffee.

"So, tell me what happened."

"The detective didn't pull punches, but Oscar was ready for him." Dottie picked up her mug. She breathed in the delicious aroma. "I'm so glad it's over."

She told Fred about the interview.

"I heard from a former colleague who runs a law firm in Savannah that Oscar Palmertree's got a reputation for being a real courtroom brawler. He'd be in his element in a situation like that. And from the sounds of it you handled yourself well."

Fred broke off a piece of pastry and popped it into his mouth. "I spoke with Rick. He'll be in the hospital for at least another week. Then he'll have to face the music." Fred dabbed his mouth with a napkin. "I'm sorry it involved you, but I'm glad he's confessed. All his life he's relied on his charm and wits to get him out of trouble."

"Let's hope this is a sign he's finally facing up to responsibilities."

"I think Virginia's made a big difference in his life," Fred said.

"Will they marry before this is all over?"

"Somehow I think he'll wait until things have settled before tying the knot." Fred smiled. "Of course, Virginia may have other ideas."

"Do you think he'll go to prison?"

"His lawyer will argue Rick acted under duress, but he'll likely do some time."

Dottie sipped her coffee and thought about the events of the last two weeks. "There are two things bothering me. The first time we went into Rick's house, we saw what looked like a bloodstain on the rug by the front door. Mabel figured it might be red paint."

"It wasn't paint. When those assholes kidnapped me, I tried to get away and got a bloodied nose for my troubles. What was the other thing?"

"That phone call you made just before we flew to Savannah. Where were you?"

"In the house where Mabel and Harriet were taken. I managed to escape and find a phone. Didn't have chance to say much. One of the goons saw me, pulled the phone out of my hand and punched me in the mouth."

They lapsed into silence for a few moments.

Dottie dabbed her lips with the paper napkin. "When's your flight?'

"Tomorrow." Fred's expression grew serious. He rested his folded arms on the table. "Dottie, after my contract in Rio is over, I'm coming to Toronto. I'd like to see you when I get back."

"I'd like that."

He smiled sheepishly. "I feel like a teenager."

They finished their coffee and pastries and left the cafe.

Fred took Dottie by the arm. "I need to tell you something." He led her to a wooden bench a few yards away and they sat down. "I've never thanked you for all you've done. Without you, I probably wouldn't be here." Fred leaned over and brushed a kiss on Dottie's lips.

Dottie felt her face grow hot. "That's what friends are for." She checked her watch. "I'm late."

When they stood up, Fred hugged her. "Look after yourself, Dottie. I'll be back before you know it."

"I hope so."

Fred smiled. "I have a request."

"What's that?"

"Scout out a good Indian restaurant so I can buy you dinner."

"You're on."

At the hotel, Mabel was waiting for her, suitcase by her side. "Dottie, you're late. We have to leave for the airport in fifteen minutes."

"We got a bit carried away. I'm packed, so all I have to do is pick up my suitcase."

Mabel's eyes grew wide. "You got carried away?"

"We didn't notice the time."

"So?"

"So what?"

Mabel smiled. "Did he propose too?"

"Of course he didn't! But we have a dinner date when he gets back to Toronto next year."

"And that's it?"

"For now."

Dottie picked up her phone. She was about to put it into her purse when she saw the text message light flashing.

It was from Hans Van Gogh, the Dutch film maker she'd met in Europe this past June. Their whirlwind romance had come to an abrupt end when Hans confessed he'd reunited with his former girlfriend.

When Dottie finished reading the message, she looked at Mabel.

"You look like the cat who swallowed the canary," Mabel said.

"Do I?"

"Well, are you going to tell me? Or what?"

"That was Hans. He and Simone have split. He's coming to Toronto next spring to shoot a documentary…He wants to see me."

"That'll put a monkey wrench in the works."

"What do you mean?"

"Fred is head over heels in love with you."

"What's that got to do with anything?"

Mabel paused. "All I'm saying is be careful. You don't want your heart broken again."

Dottie nodded. "I'll get my bag. I promised to phone Ernest, but I'll call from the airport."

"By the way, what's the documentary about?"

Dottie couldn't keep a straight face. "Drug syndicates."

The End

About Sheila Gale

Born and raised in North Wales, Sheila Gale immigrated to Canada in 1967 and spent twenty-eight years working as a college professor. After retirement, she was finally able to devote her time to her favorite pastime – writing. She's had fun with her first two books, which feature a glamorous divorcee who lusts after Harley Davidson motor bikes, and a wacky widow who loves shopping at discount stores and eating junk food.

Wintering in Hilton Head, South Carolina, with her husband of more than thirty years, she has published short stories, articles and poems in three anthologies created by the Island Writers Network.

Sheila's writers' group keeps her grounded. She's learned to leave her ego outside the door and to listen to others.

She's currently working on a mystery novel set in North Wales.

Social Media Links:

Website: www.sheilagale.ca

Facebook:

Linkedin:

Acknowledgements:

Deep gratitude to my Fiction Highway Guild critiquing group colleagues, Donna Kirk, Linda Shales and Barbara Winter for their shrewd critiques, constructive suggestions and remarkable patience; and to my readers, Michele

Fisher, Ted Gale, Jennifer Mook-Sang, and Kimberly Scutt for their insightful comments and thoughtful observations.

Heartfelt thanks to family and friends for their enthusiasm and encouragement, but most of all, to my husband Ted, for his unwavering support and his wonderful sense of humor.

Made in the USA
Charleston, SC
16 November 2016